The Elder Chronicles

Volume 6

New Breed

By

Robyn Kelly

This story is fiction. The settings are imaginary. Any resemblance of the characters or places to actual persons or places is purely coincidental.

Table of Contents

Prologue

When the Elder children assembled for their sixth session with Red Hawk, the first female shaman of the nearby Indian tribe, they found her already seated in the Council chamber. She was still wearing her traditional buckskin dress. Even seated on the floor, she was almost as tall as any of the Elders. And, as usual, she had her eyes closed as though in a trance. When her audience was duly seated and still, she slowly opened her eyes and began her tale.

"The last time we met," Red Hawk said in a calm and steady voice, "I told you how it came about that all of the Elders on Earth left this planet in the hope of reuniting with their people on their home world. Ten years have now passed and nothing has been heard from them.

"But, during this period, some other significant events took place. I continued working at the Winton hospital with no further problems. My duties eventually expanded. Besides handling the psychological and counseling cases, I began assisting Dr. Edwards. I couldn't officially become his assistant because I wasn't a medical doctor; but, whenever he wasn't comfortable in a given social or administrative situation, he called on me to stand in for him.

"Sam's detective agency continued to thrive. He added two more investigators and was able to pick and choose the cases he personally worked on.

"Most import of all my daughter, Patricia Annette Archer, was born a few months after the

Elders left Earth. Then two years later, I gave birth to a son, David Samuel Archer. Two children really put a crimp in my freewheeling ways. But, with the Elders gone, my extra-curricular activities were limited to serving the local tribe as shaman.

"Mary Gauss, whose father played such a pivotal role in our last session, disappeared from sight after his death. I could find no trace of her. But I did see an interesting article in the Winton newspaper a few months later. It seems that there was a winner of the multi-million dollar lottery that had gone unclaimed. At the last minute a lawyer showed up at the lottery office with the winning ticket. He claimed the full sum on behalf of an unnamed client of his. He never said who his client was, but I had the suspicion that the real winner was Mary Gauss.

"At the time of today's episode, Gray Wolf was aging and spent most of his time on official matters with the tribal leaders at the east end of the reservation. I split my time between the Winton Hospital and the reservation. I was always in residence at Gray Wolf's cabin on weekends. One such weekend proved especially significant.

Chapter 1

Summer Camp

It was a Sunday morning in April. Mary Gauss and her ten-year-old daughter, Joanne Elena Gauss, were lounging around their condo in Albuquerque, New Mexico. The brunch dishes were still on the counter in the kitchen. The Sunday paper was scattered about the floor. Joanne was lying on the floor, still in her pajamas, concentrating on the crossword puzzle. Mary, wearing a flowery nylon house dress with her hair still uncombed, was sitting in an over-stuffed chair looking at a magazine supplement.

"Joanne," Mary said, "take a look at this."

Joanne looked up, "What?" she asked, completely disinterested.

"This ad," Mary pointed out. She showed Joanne a half-page ad in the magazine. Joanne got up and stood beside Mary's chair to get a better look. The ad was for a summer camp.

"Summer camp! Ugh!" Joanne sneered and headed back to her spot on the floor.

"No, wait," Mary caught hold of her daughter as she was leaving "This is more than just a dude ranch summer camp. It is a working ranch where you actually get to participate in ranch activities. I seem to recall that you were rather taken by that ranch we visited last month."

Joanne hesitated. She had been taking riding lessons for a couple of years at a local stable. She

6

did enjoy being around horses, and the trip they had made to that ranch last month had been interesting. She had been able to ride around on a real western saddle while her mother and the ranch owner had been haggling over some steers. But the thought of a 'summer camp' still did not enthuse her.

"No," Joanne firmly responded. "Summer camp with a bunch of dumb city kids still sounds icky." She pulled free and went back to her spot on the floor.

"At least look at the ad," Mary persisted. "This really doesn't look like your usual summer camp. And, remember, *you're* a 'city kid'."

Joanne reluctantly returned to her mother's chair and looked. The pictures showed a corral with horses, young boys on horseback with lassos, cattle on the range. The verbiage included the typical comments: 'a unique experience for your child', 'space for only twenty ranch hands', 'real working ranch', 'special eight-week program'.

"Now does that look like your typical dude ranch?" Mary asked. "According to this you will be living together in an actual bunk house. It looks like it could be a real challenge."

Joanne still wasn't buying the whole thing and once more headed back to her crossword puzzle.

"Too challenging for you?" Mary teased. She knew her daughter only too well.

"No way!" Joanne snapped back. "Too boring!"

"Look, Jo-E.," Mary said sternly, using Joanne's current nickname. "I'm going to be devoting this summer to getting my masters in nursing. The classes are already scheduled. If you think that camp

7

would be boring, just think what it will be like around here while I'm studying and going to class. Want to take another look at that summer camp?"

Joanne's mental processes came to a skidding halt. Her mother had just invented another definition for boring. If her mother was going to be taking classes, so would she. That was her mother's favorite way of keeping Joanne occupied and out of her hair.

"Let me take another look at that ad," Joanne said. "Maybe it wouldn't be so bad after all."

There was some more discussion, and in the end Joanne agreed that she would go to the summer camp … if there were any openings left.

That presented a new and very important problem. "How long had this ad been running?" Mary wondered. "*Were* there any openings left?"

Mary got up and took the ad to the phone. There was no '800' number in the ad. The area code listed was located in southern New Mexico. Mary dialed the number. There was no answer. "Well," Mary thought, "it is a local number; and today is Sunday." She decided to try again on Monday. Then she had a second thought, "If the camp is already full, I'll have to start this process all over again! Ugh!"

Mary was working swing shift at the hospital, so she had time in the morning to try the number again. This time a kindly-sounding woman answered.

"I'd like to register my child for the summer program," Mary started. "If there are any spaces left."

The woman's reply was encouraging. "Yes," she said, "we have a few spaces left." And she began a litany of questions:

"Your Name?" "Mary Gauss."

"Address and phone number?" Mary provided the information.

"Child's name?" "Jo E. Gauss," Mary said. Then she added, "At least that's the name most of Jo E.'s friends have been using lately."

"Age?" "10"

There were a few additional questions, but nothing of consequence. Then the woman said she would be sending a detailed information packet that would include payment instructions. Full payment would have to be received at least a week before the start of the summer session. That was all there was to it.

Mary informed Joanne that she was duly registered and that the information packet would be coming in the mail. Then she hurried out to work. Joanne cleared the dishes and got busy on her current lessons.

The packet arrived in the afternoon mail a few days later. Joanne had the privilege of receiving it and opening it. It included the usual instructions, a map to the ranch, a summary of all the activities that would be taking place, ranch hands' responsibilities (really?), clothing list, a reminder to bring personal items, and a t-shirt with 'Rockin-R Ranch' and an image of the ranch's brand prominently decorating the front. Ranch hands were supposed to show up wearing the t-shirt. After examining the contents, Joanne set the packet on her mother's desk for her inspection when she got home.

9

Mary did glance at the package when she got home from work. Joanne had obviously gone through it thoroughly. Mary checked; no nasty notes. Apparently it passed muster. Mary decided she would check during breakfast, just to be sure. She also looked at the cost. "Rather steep," she thought, for what would end up being semi-slave labor by the end of the summer. Still, she could easily afford it and it would keep Joanne safely out of the way while she finished up her masters program.

At breakfast the next morning, Joanne showed up wearing her Rockin-R shirt. Mary duly noted her enthusiasm shift. "You'd better not wear that shirt out before your first day at camp," Mary cautioned. Joanne gave Mary a dirty look and took the shirt off. She was wearing one of her customary tanks beneath it. Message sent; message received.

The months until summer passed slowly for Joanne. Mary was busy working and arranging her work schedule with her summer class schedule. She gave Joanne the job of comparing her wardrobe to the camp clothing requirements and making a list of anything else she would need. Then she had to remind Joanne that her studies and regular chores came first in priority.

Joanne was managing things pretty well until she discovered that the fine print strongly suggested that the ranch hands wear western style boots. At that point Joanne made her mother very well aware that she just had to have a new pair of boots so she could get them well broken in before camp. Joanne kept pointing out that it would be a disaster if her feet blistered up on the first week of camp. And, of course, her jeans also had to be properly broken in.

As soon as Mary gave in and purchased the items, they became Joanne's daily wardrobe.

Joanne had another trick in her playbook. Whenever she went to the stables to have a riding lesson, or just practice what she had learned, Joanne made a decided effort to hang around the stable hands and get lessons in how to care for the horses. When the stable hands realized that Joanne was truly serious in her desire for knowledge, they gladly indulged her. A few of the older hands taught some special tricks for dealing with horses.

Joanne practiced her lessons by preparing and cooling down whichever horse she rode. She had gained the necessary knowledge, but was not physically strong enough to handle a standard western saddle. This began to bother her no end. No matter how much she tried to increase her strength, it just was not enough.

She took the problem to one of the younger stable hands. He listened, but had no ready solution. Joanne left the stable, somewhat dejected. At her next lesson, however, the stable hand called her aside and handed her a special catalog of western equipment. One of the items listed had been marked.

Joanne took the catalog home and explained the matter to her mother.

"Look, mother," she said, pointing to a special saddle. "This saddle is so lightweight that I could handle it easily."

Mary was sitting at the breakfast nook, nursing a cup of coffee. She looked at the saddle's description: "light weight carbon fiber forms replace the usual wood, iron or steel elements of the standard western saddle with no loss of strength or shape."

"Interesting," Mary thought and took another sip of coffee. Then she saw the price and almost choked on the coffee. Mary tried to run her household on a strict budget. The price of that saddle would blow her budget for the next three years.

"All that money for a summer camp!" she thought.

Joanne was standing right next to Mary, expectantly waiting for her decision. Mary was really beginning to regret pushing the whole summer camp idea . "Oh, well, she thought, it's just money."

"Okay, Jo E.", she gave in, "you can have your saddle."

After that things went so smoothly that, before either Mary or Joanne realized it, it was time for Joanne to go to camp.

Chapter 2

No Girls Allowed

Mary and Joanne were up well before the sun on the first day of camp. Mary had suggested that they drive down to Las Cruces on Sunday and then have a short drive over to the ranch on Monday morning. But Joanne wanted a last day of riding just before they left. Mary's comment that Joanne would be saddle sore in a week anyway, was not well received. So it was they found themselves driving along the interstate as the sun rose behind them. After a quick stop in Deming for fuel and breakfast, they were on their way again.

"Are you following the map?" Mary asked. "I thought the turn-off for the ranch was somewhere along here."

"I'm trying to," Joanne answered. "But it's confusing and the signs aren't all that clear." Joanne turned the map she was holding around for the third time. "Oh, wait!" she yelled. "We just passed the turn!"

"What!?" Mary was more than a bit agitated.

"Don't worry," Joanne assured her. "Just turn around here and take the next left."

Mary executed the maneuver, driving carefully through the median. She was thankful there were no state police observing her illegal activity. At the intersection she obediently turned left and drove slowly along the side road for another ten miles. Suddenly, Joanne called out, "There it is!"

Indeed, there it was; a mailbox and a large wooden gate set back from the road with a sign hanging over it the proudly announcing, 'Rockin-R Ranch', bounded by a pair of Rockin-R brands. Mary turned right onto the narrow road that led under the gate. It was not yet 8:30.

The road leading into the ranch was bounded on both sides by white wooden fencing. The fields beyond the fences were grassy, but seemed to be lacking in any animal life. The road went on for a good two hundred yards then broadened out into an open space containing a large two-story wooden house, also painted white. There were a couple of trees and some flower beds in front and limited space for parking. There was also a small temporary sign which said, 'Ranch Hand Sign-in' with an arrow pointing to the left.

Mary slowed even more and cautiously turned to the left around the house. There was another larger sign next to the house that said, 'Ranch Hand Sign-in' with no arrow. It was obvious that incoming cars were expected to park next to house at that location. There were no other cars parked in the area. Mary duly turned in toward the house and parked. She and Joanne got out, stretched and looked around.

Farther on, beyond the house were some other out-buildings. Then, even farther were a corral and large barn. To Joanne's delight, there were several horses visible in the corral. Mary almost had to restrain her physically to keep her from running off.

"I think we are supposed to register first," Mary said. "This looks like the office." And Mary led Joanne to a door in the side of the house with a sign above it that read, 'OFFICE'. The inner wooden

14

door was open with an outer screen door protecting the interior from unwanted pests. Mary knocked tentatively on the screen door.

"Come in," came from the inside. The warm and inviting voice was obviously male. Mary and Joanne went in.

"Please, sit down," the man said, standing to greet the newcomers. "I am Glenn Rogers, owner of the Rockin-R. I take it that one of you is going to be a ranch hand here for the summer."

"I am," Joanne piped up. She was appropriately clad in her ranch shirt, blue jeans, cowboy boots and hat.

"I am Mary Gauss," Mary introduced herself. "And this is, Jo E."

"Well, let's see … " Mr. Rogers said as he sat back down and thumbed through a pile of index cards. "Yes, indeed, I do have a ranch hand by the name of Joey, who has signed on for the summer. Everything seems to be in order, all paid up. So," He stood up and extended his hand to Joanne, "welcome to the Rockin-R, Mr. Gauss."

Joanne and Mary both looked up at that last utterance. "I am a 'miss', not a 'mister'!" Joanne replied with some emphasis.

"What?" Mr. Rogers said. He simultaneously dropped Joanne's hand like a hot potato and took a step back. "That's impossible. All of our ranch hands are boys." He continued backing up until he plopped into the chair by his desk.

"Well," Mary said, slightly smiling. "It looks like you have just broken through the gender barrier."

"No, no," Mr. Rogers protested. "You don't understand. We are simply not equipped to cope with young girls. I will have to refund your money. I'm sorry you made the trip here in vain."

"Not so fast," Mary interjected. She had sudden nightmares of all her carefully laid plans for the summer going up in flames, not to mention that incredibly expensive saddle. "You just said that I had paid in full for the summer session and that everything was in order. We have a contract here and you aren't going to break it without a fight."

"My dear lady," Mr. Rogers explained, "we are only equipped to deal with boys here. The fact that 'Joey' is a girl is simply not acceptable. It was you who invalidated the contract by not initially disclosing that your child was a girl."

But Mary was just getting started – she had a lot more to lose than Glenn Rogers did. Joanne had been listening to this and showing all the signs that she expected to lose out on her summer vacation. Mary motioned her to be calm and pulled out a file folder she had brought with her.

"Mr. Rogers," Mary continued, "I have here a copy of the ad to which I responded. It says nothing about 'boys' or 'girls'. It exclusively uses the word 'child'. When I called up to register, your secretary never did ask for the gender of my child. The material you sent us in your 'information package' is also silent on any reference to gender. You haven't got a leg to stand on."

Glenn Rogers was beginning to get flustered. He was used to getting his own way and this woman was becoming a real pain. "I take it," he protested sarcastically, "that your husband is a contract lawyer, Mrs. Gauss."

"I am not a '*Mrs.*', Mr. Rogers," Mary interjected. "And kindly keep your opinions to yourself," she added. "I am fully capable of suing you for enough money to shut this ranch down. And I have lawyers on retainer who can do just that."

Joanne was smiling at her mother's feistiness. Even if she eventually lost this was a good show.

"Now, *Ms.* Gauss," Mr. Rogers was not through, yet. "My wife recorded your child's name as, 'Joey', clearly a boys name. I hardly think that was an error. If it was, it's the first one she has ever made."

"Mr. Rogers," Mary explained. "My child's full name is 'Joanne Elena'. As I indicated to the person I called, her friends call her, 'Jo E.'. I was not asked to spell it.

"It appears that two assumptions were made. Your wife assumed that 'Joey' was a boys name and asked no further questions. I assumed that you accepted *any* child into your ranch-hands camp. I couldn't imagine that you would discriminate against *children*."

"Ms. Gauss," Mr. Rogers tried again. "I do not *discriminate* against children. But the ranch just isn't equipped to deal with boys *and* girls. There are privacy concerns. And we have no time to make any changes this year. If you want, we can make some changes over the winter and you can come back next summer."

Mary was not going to be put off. "Just what kind of 'privacy concerns' are we talking about here?"

"Well, for starters," Mr. Rogers started ticking off all the problem areas, "The showers and the toilets in the bunkhouse are communal. There are no doors and no curtains. The wash basins are just a pair of troughs outside the bunkhouse. Everyone sleeps together in an open area. Again, no doors and no curtains. We are going to be out on the range for most of the summer. There aren't any toilets out there at all. Baths, if any, will be in a pond or river. Changing clothes will be done out in the open ..."

"And your concern is ... ?" Mary asked

"Why, that is just not a proper environment for a young girl," Mr. Rogers said emphatically.

"Do you really feel that she could be physically harmed?" Mary persisted. " Have you no control over the male ranch hands around here?"

"Oh, no," he answered. "I have no doubt about her physical safety. It just isn't a 'proper' environment for a young lady."

"Do you have any other objections?" Mary asked.

"Isn't that enough?" Mr. Rogers was getting exasperated. He heard another car pulling into the parking lot. He had to get rid of this woman.

"Alright," Mary stated evenly, "I trust my daughter. Why don't we let Joanne decide if she wants to spend the summer with no privacy and a bunch of smelly boys."

Glenn Rogers could hear footsteps on the gravel outside the door. He wanted desperately to end this conversation. 'Okay," he said.

Mary turned to Joanne, who had been paying close attention to all that had gone on. "Well, dear,"

Mary asked her daughter, "how do you feel about all this lack of privacy."

"Actually, Mom," Joanne calmly answered, 'it sounds a lot less funky than those nudist camps we go to all the time. I think it will be a blast! Now, can I go down to the corral and look at the horses?"

Glenn Rogers almost bit his cigar in two. He had no further arguments. "Alright," he reluctantly agreed. Then he turned his attention to Joanne. "Stow your gear in the bunkhouse. There is a list of the daily activities posted in the dining hall. Don't be late to any of them. I would still love an excuse to send you home!"

Mary had a few more pointed words for Mr. Rogers, then she and Joanne left the office.

In the parking lot, Mary and Joanne ran into another woman with child in tow heading for the office. One glance at the 'child' and it was clear she also was a girl. On a whim, Mary said to the other mother, "May I speak to you for a minute?" When the woman paused, Mary added, "Let's step over here."

While they were speaking, Joanne introduced herself. "Hi," she said, "My name's Joanne, but my friends call me 'Jo E.'. What's yours?"

"My name is Roberta," the girl answered. "But most people call me 'Bobbi'."

"Okay, Bobbi. I'm going over to the bunkhouse now," Joanne said. "Want to be bunk mates?"

"Sure!"

Their brief chat was cut short by the return of Mary and Bobbi's mother.

"Come on, Bobbi, let's go get registered," Bobbi's mother said.

When the two entered the office, Joanne could hear the woman introduce herself through the screen door, "Good morning, Mr. Rogers. I am Mrs. Arnold, and this is my daughter, Bobbi."

Joanne took her duffle bag and saddle out of the car and bade her mother good-bye as the latter headed back to Albuquerque. Then Joanne took off down the hill toward the dining hall and bunkhouse. "Things are really looking up," she thought.

Chapter 3

How to Pick a Horse

On her way to the bunkhouse, Joanne had to pass by the dining hall. As she was going by, she remembered Mr. Rogers' edict that the activity list would be posted in the dining hall and she had better not be late to any event. She wandered over to the front door and tried it. It opened easily.

Joanne put her duffle bag and saddle down by the entrance and went inside. There was one large room containing six small tables with four chairs at each one and a larger table against a side wall. All the tables appeared to be set for lunch. Joanne looked around. There on the wall by the front door was the bulletin board. And on the bulletin board was the activity list. Joanne scanned the page ...

8:00-11:00 Sign-in

12:00-1:00 Lunch

4:00 Bunk Check

6:00 Supper

8:00 Campfire

10:00 Lights out

The entry for 'bunk check' was a puzzle, but the others were clear enough. It was barely 9:00, so there was plenty of time for horses before noon.

Joanne had another mission while she was in the dining room. She headed back to the kitchen and peeked in. Happily it was empty. She went in and located the refrigerator. Opening it up, she rummaged around a bit until she found a bowl of carrots, obviously waiting to become part of the noon salad. Joanne picked out a couple of small ones. Then she returned to the main room and went over to a table where she helped herself to a few sugar cubes from a convenient bowl.

Thus armed, Joanne retrieved her duffle bag and saddle and headed for the bunkhouse. On her way she passed the 'troughs'. They were indeed two metal troughs with a wooden shelf mounted above them and water spigots spaced out along them. There was an attempt at a roof overhead with a branch off toward the bunkhouse. Wooden planks were laid out along the ground to keep the ranch hands' feet out of the mud.

Joanne followed the roof to a gaping doorway in the end of the bunkhouse. Inside was an open area containing showers to the right and toilets to the left. As advertised, there we no stalls. There were, however, small walls between each of the toilets. "Somewhere to hang the toilet paper," Joanne thought.

Straight through the shower area was the main room with the bunk beds, five of them on each side. There was a large locker on either side of each bunk. On each bunk was a rolled up mattress, blanket, sheets, pillow, pillowcase towel and washcloth. Apparently, Joanne was the first ranch hand to make it this far.

Joanne was about to lay claim to a bunk when Bobbi arrived through the front door. She was quite out of breath and dragging a large suitcase behind her.

"Hi," Joanne called. "Any preference as to bunk?"

Bobbi pulled her suitcase over to where Joanne was standing. "I've never done anything like this before," she confided. "What do you suggest?"

"Well," Joanne pondered the situation. "Since all eyes are going to be on us anyway, one of these on the end would probably be the best bet. How about this one?" Joanne indicated a bunk on the front of the bunkhouse next to the shower room. "Do you want top or bottom?"

"Oh, the top kinda scares me," Bobbi answered. "Can I have the bottom?"

"Sure," Joanne said. "I'll take the locker on the inside and you can have the locker by the door."

Joanne proceeded to unload her duffle bag into her locker in accordance with a diagram posted on the inside of the locker door. Once it was empty, she rolled up the duffle bag and stowed it on top of the locker. Bobbi did the same with her belongings. Joanne helped Bobbi heave the empty suitcase onto the top of her locker. Joanne then shoved her saddle out of sight under the bunk.

Joanne spread out the mattress on the top bunk and coached Bobbi in the proper way to make up a bunk. She wrapped two sheets and a blanket around it and tucked everything in securely. A pillow in pillowcase at the head of the bed next to the wall completed the ensemble. Except for the towel and washcloth, which ended up neatly folded over the bedrail at the foot of the bed. Bobbi duplicated Joanne's effort.

Joanne and Bobbi looked over their work and pronounced it good enough. "Now let's go check out the horses!" Joanne exclaimed.

As the two girls left the bunkhouse they saw a few of the boys coming down the hill from the ranch house. They didn't bother to wait for them but ran straight over to the corral. Joanne immediately climbed up to the top rail and sat down. Bobbi joined her. The two girls just sat there and watched as the horses milled about.

There were all sorts and sizes of horses. Several pintos, a palomino, a couple of roans, one larger black horse and a few non-descript. Joanne wasn't sure, but she thought she saw a burro over on the far side of the corral.

"How do you pick out the right horse?" Bobbi asked.

"You don't pick out the horse," Joanne answered. "The horse picks you out."

"What?" Bobbi was totally confused.

"Watch," was all Joanne said. She continued to sit quietly on the top rail looking at the horses. She silently sent out a welcoming thought, then added the thought of a carrot.

The horses continued to mill around aimlessly. Then one little pinto, just Joanne's size slowly began to approach her. Still, Joanne waited patiently. The pinto stopped and turned back into the herd. "Didn't feel right'" Joanne mumbled. Joanne and Bobbi continued to wait until a larger roan passed by Bobbi and slowed to a stop in font of Joanne.

Joanne slowly reached into her pocket for a carrot, broke it in half and offered a piece to the roan who accepted it gladly. Next came a piece of sugar. The deal was sealed! Several of the boys came up just in time to see Joanne stand up on the fence and slip onto the roan's back.

Joanne spent the next fifteen minutes riding the roan bareback around the corral. Her ride only came to an end when the whoops and hollers from the boys attracted the attention of Bill Thomas, the ranch hands' foreman and camp counselor. He came up to the corral to see what all the excitement was and immediately shouted for Joanne to get off the horse. His shout startled Joanne and she immediately dropped off the horse's back – right in the middle of the corral. All of this excitement agitated the other horses and they began to move about much more skittishly.

Now Bill was more worried than ever and climbed up the corral fence in an effort to intervene and rescue this stupid ranch hand. Joanne, on the other hand, practically invisible in the sea of horses, was gently patting each of the horses near her. The simple attention calmed down those around her and that calmness spread to the rest. By the time Bill made it to the top of the corral fence, all was quiet again. Joanne noted his appearance and maneuvered over to where he was sitting.

"Thanks for spoiling my fun and scaring all the horses," Joanne's sarcasm was showing.

"What you did was very dangerous," Bill scolded. "You could have been badly hurt."

"Oh, posh!" Joanne shot back. "I knew exactly what I was doing. By the way what is that roan's name? I would like to ride her this summer. That is, if no one else has a claim on her. The horse and I have an understanding." Joanne climbed up the fence and straddled the top rail.

"An understanding?" Bill was amazed. "That's the first time I ever heard that one." After a moment he replied almost absentmindedly, "That horse is called 'Molly'".

"Wait a minute," Bill added as he realized to whom he was speaking. "You're a girl! What are you even doing here at the corral?"

"I guess you didn't get the memo," Joanne just knew she was going to enjoy this. "The Rockin-R has gone co-ed. Bobbi and I are two of your new ranch hands."

The silence was deafening. Bill stared. The other boys stared. Bobbi wanted to run and hide.

Bill looked alternately at Joanne and Bobbi. "You two are ranch hands?" he was absolutely dumfounded.

"Oh, Bill, say it ain't so!" one of the boys chimed in.

"'Fraid so, guys," Joanne said, smiling. "Oh, look at the time," she added. "It's almost noon. I wouldn't want to be late for lunch. Come on, Bobbi." She and Bobbi jumped down from the fence and started up the hill to the dining room.

Lunch that day consisted of a small salad – less a couple of carrots – cold sandwiches and milk to drink. "Healthy," Joanne supposed, "but hardly inspiring." Bill Thomas and Mr. Rogers ate with the ranch hands. They were seated at the long table. After lunch, Mr. Rogers welcomed all the ranch hands and introduced Bill as the summer counselor. Bill would be sleeping in the bunk house with the ranch hands and would be in charge. Any problems were to be taken to him.

Then Mr. Rogers paused. He seemed to be looking for just the right words. He apparently failed to find them for he simply blurted out that this summer there would be two girls joining the ranch hands. They would be living in the bunk house and sharing all the facilities. Then he told everyone to have an enjoyable summer and beat a hasty retreat before the initial excitement over his last pronouncement could result in a slew of very uncomfortable questions. Those were left for Bill to answer.

No matter what the question, Bill's answer was always the same: "We have two girls with us this summer, they will be living in the bunkhouse, just treat them the same way you would treat any other boys."

Then Bill lapsed into a series of general instructions regarding how to make up the bunks, how to stow personal belongings, and – most important of all – not to forget to sign up for dining hall service. The sign-up sheet, he pointed out was on the end of the head table. After that, he suggested that they all get over to the bunk house and get ready for bunk inspection at 4:00.

By the time Joanne and Bobbi got to the head table to sign up, most of the boys had beat them to it The only spaces open were in the second month. Well, by then, Joanne figured they would have plenty of time to find out what this was all about. Then she and Bobbi moseyed back to the bunkhouse.

Chapter 4

Bunkhouse Standoff

When they got to the bunkhouse, Joanne and Bobbi first stopped off at the toilets then went into the main room. It was a bee-hive of activity. All of the boys were struggling to put away their personal items and make their beds and stow their suitcases. Joanne and Bobbie just stretched out on Bobbi's bunk and watched the show. A few of the older, more experienced boys were helping the younger first-timers. By 4:00 most everything was in readiness when Bill walked in to begin the 'Bunk Check'.

"The whole purpose of this exercise," Bill explained, "is to ensure that each one of you is properly equipped for the summer ahead of us. And that you have a basic knowledge of how to make a bed and the ability to do it. I am going to count on you old-timers to help the tenderfeet get things organized. Now, let's see how you have done."

With that, Bill started down the row of bunks. In most cases, everything passed muster. Where it didn't, he would suggest a correction. As he approached Joanne and Bobbi they jumped off the bunk where they had been lying and straightened the blanket. When Bill arrived, he gave their work a quick glance. Then he gave it a more thorough examination. He poked here and there in the lockers, checked the tightness of the blankets on the beds. He finally decided that their bags should be placed on the floor under the bed. They could fall off the top of the lockers.

Joanne glanced down the row of bunks; over half the boys had bags of various sorts on top of their lockers. "Ahem,' Joanne interrupted. "What about those?" she pointed at the other lockers.

"Well," Bill said weakly, "those boys are older."

"Toby is about half my age," Joanne pointed out.

"Toby is nine years old." Bill asserted. "He's just small. Now please take the bags down."

"But, we're just little girls," Joanne tossed back. "We might get hurt if we did that."

Bill was obviously irritated, but he agreed, just to make his point. "I'll get them down," he said and pulled the two bags off the lockers and put them on the bottom bunk.

"But where should we put them?" Bobbi asked. "They won't fit in the lockers."

"Put them under the bunk!" Bill was sorry he had started this; but he had to finish it.

"Bobbi's suitcase won't fit; it's too big," Joanne said as she slid her duffle bag under the bunk. She was happy to be helpful.

"Well," Bill answered, addressing himself to Joanne, "You're so smart, you figure it out." "Don't forget," he announced as he turned and left the bunkhouse, "Supper at six and there is a campfire afterwards."

Joanne and Bobbi just looked at the suitcase for a couple of minutes. Joanne was aware that the boys were watching to see what they were going to do.

"Come on, Bobbi," Joanne said, "Grab hold." The two took hold of the suitcase and heaved it back on top of the locker.

"Hey, you can't do that," one of the older boys said. "Bill said that was too dangerous for girls." He drew out the word 'girls' as a derisive taunt.

"We'll take our chances," Bobbi chimed. "Besides, it's my suitcase. And *you* are safe."

"Doesn't matter?" the boy replied. "I'm Bill's assistant, and I say you got to take it down."

"Since when?" Joanne challenged.

"Since now," the boy demanded.

"And what if we don't believe you?" Bobbi asked.

"You'd better believe it!" A second boy added. Then he made a fatal mistake. "You're just girls and you have to do what we say," he added.

"Didn't you hear Mr. Rogers say at lunch that we are supposed to get along?" Joanne asked.

"We'll get along all right," a third boy got in on the act. "So long as you do what we tell you to do."

Bobbi was beginning to be intimidated by the boys' strident attitude. But Joanne wasn't ready to bend an inch. "That isn't going to happen," she said evenly. "Just get over it."

"What?" The first boy asked. "You going to make us?"

There was general laughter and guffaws from the boys. The whole group was beginning to approach Joanne and Bobbi, boxing them into a corner.

"I don't have to 'make you' do anything," Joanne said. "I am just going to ignore you. And, I trust, you will ignore Bobbi and me. There's no reason we can't get along."

"I think you need a lesson to teach you your proper place," the first boy threatened.

"Yeah," a second boy sounded off, "around here, when there is a disagreement, we settle the issue with boxing gloves."

"Boxing gloves are so cumbersome and ineffective," Joanne taunted. "Are you big strong boys afraid to tackle one measly little girl, '*mano-a-mano*'? You want to make me, bring it on!"

"That go for your girlfriend, too?" A voice from the crowd asked.

Joanne was just standing casually at the end of her bunk as though she hadn't a care in the world.

"I'm just speaking for me," Joanne answered. "But, if any of you try to harm Bobbi, you'll have to go through me first."

"Oooh, I'm afraid!" Came from one of the boys.

Joanne looked around to ensure that no one was sneaking up behind her. She moved carefully along the side of her bunk.

"If you're hopin' Bill will be back," one of the boys piped up. "We won't see him again until supper."

"Well," Joanne tried again. "I can keep up this banter for another hour, if I have to, but it's really getting quite boring. So why don't you children just go back to minding your own business and Bobbi and I will do the same."

"I think she needs a spanking," came from the crowd. That was followed by a number of hoots and hollers of support.

"What do you say," the first boy asked Joanne. "You want a spanking?"

"Try it, if think you can do it," Joanne said evenly. She was still standing casually with no sign of fear or tenseness. "Oh, by the way," she added, "What name do we put on your tombstone?"

"I'm Tim," the first boy said.

"And I am Rodney," the second boy said. "There won't be enough of you left to bother burying."

"Get her!" came from the crowd.

Tim lunged for Joanne with Rodney right behind him. Two seconds later they were both lying on the floor groaning in pain. Neither Bobbi nor any of the other boys could have explained what happened.

In point of fact, in the first second, Joanne stepped beside Tim as he charged, grabbed his arm and used his own momentum to fling him around between the uprights at the end of the bunk and onto the floor beyond. Then, in the next second, Joanne spun around and, taking advantage of the momentum of her own spin, chopped Rodney across the throat with her hand while simultaneously taking his feet out from under him. He sprawled on the floor gasping for breath. Joanne wasn't even breathing hard.

Then, Joanne turned her attention to the crowd of boys standing there with their mouths open. "Any one else want to give me a spanking?" She asked sweetly.

There were no takers as the boys soberly broke up their little mob. Joanne called to a couple of them to pick up their friends and put them on their bunks.

Joanne remained casually standing beside her bunk, carefully watching in case the festivities should resume. Bobbi climbed up on her bunk, leaned over the edge and quietly asked Joanne, "How?"

Joanne just smiled and softly answered, "Aikido."

Bill, who had been clandestinely watching from a rear window, just in case he might need to intervene, decided the situation had been properly resolved. He moved off to report to Mr. Rogers.

Just before 6:00, when the ranch hands would be going to supper, Joanne walked up to the other end of the bunkhouse, where Tim and Rodney were recovering. The boys were rather leery when she approached and tended to move back a bit.

Joanne stopped beside Tim's bunk, stretched out her hand, and said, "I'm really sorry our little misunderstanding got so out of hand. I hope we can all get along in the future."

Tim still wasn't sure what had happened, but he was certain he did not want to repeat the experience. He took the extended hand and said, "Things did sorta get out of control. I'm all for getting along in the future."

Joanne reached up to Rodney on the top bunk with the same message. He, too, took the proffered hand and agreed to get along in the future.

Bill and Mr. Rogers arrived early at the dining hall in anticipation of a problem situation. To their surprise, the entire ranch hand crew came in right on time, laughing and joking with each other. Good feeling definitely prevailed. The fight was over, but it would not be forgotten for some time. In the future, Bobbi and Joanne would be treated as just two more ranch hands.

Chapter 5

Open Range

Right after breakfast the next morning, the horses were assigned. As she requested, Joanne got Molly. Needless to say, everyone was surprised when she showed up with her own saddle. Then the saddle became the object of attention. It was so light weight that Bill didn't think it was safe to use. It took Joanne several minutes to convince him that it was made of carbon fiber with a waterproof leather over-wrap. The younger boys needed help to handle their standard western saddles, but Joanne was able to handle hers with ease.

As Joanne was putting her saddle on Molly, Tim walked by and whispered, "Money!" To which Joanne replied in the same tone, "Yeah!"

Joanne had demonstrated that she could saddle and bridle her horse without assistance. Charlie, the stable master who was helping the other ranch hands, checked her work and remarked that she did a 'right good job'.

Once the horses were saddled, the ranch hands had to demonstrate their proficiency at riding. In most cases 'proficiency' simply meant that they didn't fall off their horse every few minutes. To everyone's surprise, Joanne and Bobbi were among the better riders, even among the returning ranch hands.

Two groups were formed. The younger and less experienced riders stayed with Charlie for a day or two until they could perform better on horseback.

Bill took the more proficient riders out for a ride around the ranch. These first days, everyone came together at the ranch for lunch and supper. But, before the ranch hands could go to supper, they had to curry, feed and otherwise tend to their horses. Thanks to the instruction from her friends at the Albuquerque stables, Joanne proved equally proficient at this chore.

As soon as everyone could sit their horse well, the rides gradually became longer and longer. The ranch hands would get a bag lunch and a canteen at breakfast and take off for the day. They got to see all sorts of grazing grounds from the sparse desert areas close to the ranch to the more verdant on some of the distant hills. Bill made sure that they learned the location of the various wells and ponds where they could water their horses, and, in some cases, themselves.

During these rides, life on the ranch became much more interesting. But Joanne was still wondering where all of the 'working ranch' was happening. Finally, at one rest stop, she cornered Bill …

"Bill, the riding around has been fun," Joanne asked between bites of hotdog, "but aren't we supposed to take part in ranch activities? When and where is that going to happen?"

"Well," Bill replied slowly and deliberately, "that will begin next week. You see, the main herd is a lot farther out, farther away from the ranch house than we have ridden so far. You may have noticed that there aren't any real ranch hands bunked in by the house. This time of year they all live and work out on the open range. Before we can join them, we have to be sure that all of the kids are up to riding as much as it takes to get to the herd and then ride along with it."

"Oh!" was all that Joanne could muster. She wandered away from Bill and sought out Tim.

Joanne and Tim had not exactly become fast friends, but they did have a healthy respect for each other. She found Tim and a couple of the older boys sharing lunch together and sat down beside him.

"Tim," Joanne began when she got the chance to break into the conversation, "you've come the Rockin-R before haven't you?"

Tim looked over at Joanne and wondered what she was up to this time. "Yeah," he answered carefully, "this is my third year."

"What's it like when we actually get to go out with the working ranch hands?" Joanne asked.

"What do you mean?" Tim was still suspicious.

"All this riding around was fun at first," Joanne said evenly, "but it is beginning to get boring. We don't seem to be getting any ranch experience. I was just wondering … "

"Oh, you'll get experience all right," Tim confided. "Right now, Bill is just getting the new kids used to riding. Starting next Monday we will head out as usual with a lunch, but we will end up eating supper with the crew out on the range. We sleep out in the open, rain or shine, and spend the week helping them with whatever they are doing at the moment.

"Last year," Tim continued, "we got in on the tail end of the branding. Our job was to search for wayward young calves and doggies in the outlying scrub and move them back into the branding area."

"You mean lasso them?" Joanne asked cautiously. She thought that might be fun, but it could also be very dangerous.

"No," Tim answered, "you are too inexperienced for that." Even as he said it, Tim watched Joanne carefully, almost expecting her to explode at the thought that she might be inexperienced at something. But she remained calmly seated, so he continued.

"Rod and I are older and we have had two years' experience. They *might* let us do some roping this year, if we beg hard enough.

"You'll just let your horse move the calf around. They are trained for that. You just hang on and let the horse do the work. Then, for the rest of the summer, we will just stay with the ranch crew, one week at a time, helping them do whatever they are doing. During the last couple of weeks, we will join the crew as they move the cattle that are to be sold down to the pasture next to the rail spur."

"Thanks, Tim," Joanne said as she got up. "That's just what I was looking for." As Joanne left, Rodney, who was seated nearby, looked over at Tim questioningly. Tim just shrugged and shook his head.

When Joanne returned to Bobbi, the latter asked, "What did you find out?"

"Ill tell you tonight," Joanne said. "It looks like we are going to get started again."

"Oh, my aching bottom!" Bobbi said as she struggled to her feet. Bobbi knew how to handle a horse, but she was not used to long hours on horseback.

As the week went on, Joanne and Bobbi learned just how hard it was going to be. The rides were harder and lasted longer. And the ranch hands were gradually getting tougher. By the end of that first week, they all felt they had earned sufficient calluses for the work that would be coming.

On Sunday there was a church service in the dining hall after breakfast. Joanne didn't bother attending. That caused a few raised eyebrows, but no one had the courage to say anything. That afternoon, the ranch hands gathered at the stable where each was issued a bed roll, poncho, saddle bags and a canteen. Then Bill gave them a list of things to bring with them on Monday morning. The rest of that afternoon was spent doing the laundry. There was a big campfire in the evening where, among the usual songs, the exploits, both great and funny, of the past week were recounted.

Early Monday morning they set off, riding north at first, then turning a bit to the east. They rode steadily all day, pausing only for lunch and an occasional pit stop. It was beginning to get dark when they sighted the fires at the ranch crew's camp. Bill greeted the men at the camp and made arrangements for his ranch hands to bed down nearby. The crew was ready for them and had extra chow on the fire.

Joanne and the others staked out their horses near the water source, gave them a rubdown , and fed them. They took their bedrolls and saddles over to their designated spot and laid them out. Then everyone made a bee line for a very tasty meal of beans and beef.

After supper, the crew leader explained that they were out there to brand the last of the new calves.

"Most ranches that tightly control their cattle," he said, "just use ear tags or tattoos. They are considered to be much more humane and more accurate. But the Rockin'-R and another nearby ranch have free range cattle, as you will see tomorrow. In such cases it is important that those of us who are handling the cattle be able to see at a glance from horseback to whom each animal belongs. So we are out here placing old fashioned brands on each Rockin-R animal."

Even after a hard day's ride, that first night spent sleeping on the hard ground with just a poncho and horse blanket for protection was not the most comfortable. Joanne, and several of the other ranch hands, reported dreams of hot branding irons and seared flesh.

After a fair night's sleep, a visit to the crew's latrine and a quick breakfast of coffee and biscuits the ranch hands got their introduction to the branding operation.

As Tim had predicted, the crew used the ranch hands to locate and drive out any leftover calves. The ranch hands were split into two groups. One watched the branding and the other hunted for wayward calves. Joanne, Bobbi, Tim and Rodney along with a few other experienced riders made their way through the brush looking for calves that might be hiding there. Molly almost stumbled on one calf lying quietly in some tall grass. Joanne used her lasso to prod the calf into rising, then Molly guided the calf out into the open where Bobbi was waiting.

In the afternoon, following a lunch consisting of simple sandwiches and warm soft drinks, the morning group of ranch hands got to go over to the fire pit where the crew was working and watch them brand the calves. Those who had watched the branding in the morning were sent out to the scrub brush to hunt for more calves.

At the branding site, a crew member pointed out that the calf protested a whole lot more before the brand was applied than after.

"Like a kid about the get a shot from the doctor," he explained. "The kid always yells louder before he gets the shot than after. I ought to know – I got four of them."

After watching a few get branded, Joanne had to agree. It was a scary process, and she was sure that she never wanted to get branded, but it looked like it really did the animal very little harm.

The ranch hands spent the rest of the week moving with the crew. The number of calves dwindled, until, at the end of the week, they could not find one all afternoon.

Saturday they made the ride back to the ranch. Every one was glad to finally be able to take a shower and spend two whole nights in a bed. They had another campfire Sunday night. They spent the time singing songs and recounting stories of their exploits out on the range. Including the time one of the younger ranch hands leaned over a little too far while moving a calf out of the brush and ended up riding out of the brush on the calf's back.

On Monday they were off to check out the breeding process.

This time they met the crew at the main herd. There were thousands of cattle spread out along a green lowland between two mountain ranges. The crew rode through the herd marking the cows they wanted to breed with orange spray paint. The ranch hands would follow them and cut out as many of the marked cows as would oblige them. If a cow proved reticent, one of the crew would use his lasso or a cattle prod to encourage it to do as it was told.

While the ranch hands were cutting out the cows, Tim happened to ride by Joanne and whispered, "I hope you have already had Sex Ed 101." He quickly rode off before she could reply.

The cows that were cut out were moved into a large temporary steel corral that had been erected off to one side. When Joanne was relieved from cutting duty, she got to go over to the corral and watch the insemination process. It was remarkably simple and quick.

One or two crew members working in the corral would select a cow and move her into a long chute extending from the side of the corral opposite the gate. Occasionally a cow, who had been through this process before, wanted no part of it. If she got too balky she would be encouraged to move along with a not-so-gentle whack on the rear or a cattle prod in the same location. Once in the chute, the walls of the chute would be closed against the cow to hold her in place. At that point a crew member would approach the cow from behind, hold her tail up and insert a long slender tube into her vagina. A quick push of the plunger and the job was done. The cow was then marked with a shot of blue paint, the chute walls were relaxed, the gate at the end of the chute opened and the cow escaped back into the herd.

One of the crew members explained that the tube contained semen from a carefully selected bull.

"We have about a 95% success rate from this process," he said. "It does the cow no harm, and about 240 days or so from now, when the weather starts turning warm, she will drop a nice healthy new calf."

Joanne was thoroughly intrigued by the process. Once she had seen the actual insemination, she observed the preparation for the process. Two or three of the metal tubes were kept on a table by the chute. As one tube was used, another would be brought up to replace it and the used tube would be carried off.

Joanne followed the crew member of was managing the tubes. He moved between the corral and a box truck that was parked nearby. The back of the truck was open. Inside Joanne could see a large circular container and a generator. The generator was humming steadily.

The crew member tossed the used tubes into a box and lifted the lid of the circular container. As he did so, a small cloud emanated from the container. He put on a glove, removed one or two tubes from the container and quickly sealed it. He put the tubes in a small cloth sack, removed the glove, and carried the sack back to the corral.

The whole process began to fascinate Joanne. She shadowed the crew member who was shuttling the tubes around and asked him what it was all about.

"I take it you haven't seen the bull 'milking' process?" he asked.

"No, not yet," Joanne replied.

"Well, you probably will," he offered. "Our job is to take the bull's semen and process it to extract as much of the sperm as possible. Then we separate the sperm into several batches, each sufficient to impregnate a cow, and store each batch in a tube. The tubes are then frozen with liquid nitrogen in this 'cryo' unit until they are needed. Once I take a tube out of the 'cryo' unit, it will thaw to a usable state by the time I walk it over to the corral."

Joanne thanked him for the information and wandered back to the corral.

That was only a third of the process. Later in the week, the ranch hands got to watch as the young males were separated into bulls and steers. The young males that were selected to live their lives among the ranch stud herd were cut out by the ranch crew members and transferred to a separate meadow where they would have no contact with any of the cows.

Those males who would be raised solely for beef were rounded up into a similar type of steel corral and processed out one at a time through a chute. In their case, however, the process was considerably more drastic. While they were in the chute, a veterinarian would deaden their scrotum, slice it open and surgically remove the testicles. The newly made steer would then spend its life in the herd with the females.

For some reason, the boys tended to look at the castration process with some dread and uneasiness. For Joanne and Bobbi it was fascinating.

Part three of the process took place in the bulls' pasture. Before the ranch hands were allowed into the bulls' pasture they were warned to ride slowly and deliberately around the herd. While the bulls were usually docile enough to be safe, they were full of testosterone and could act violently without a moment's notice. When Joanne and Bobbi got a look at the large size of the bulls, they were especially wary. There was another steel corral in this pasture, but it had been significantly modified.

The corral was smaller, but appeared sturdier. There was also a chute opposite the gate, but the end of it had been blocked off. When Joanne commented on it one of the crew referred to the end of the chute as 'Betsy'. Upon close examination, Joanne had to agree that it did look something like the south end of a north-bound cow.

The ranch hands, those who wanted to anyway, were give a chance to watch the 'milking' of the bulls. Three or four select bulls at a time were rounded up into the corral. Then one at a time they were ushered into the chute. One of the crew would spray Betsy with a pheromone concoction. As soon as the bull got a whiff of that he would rear up and mount Betsy the same way he would mount a cow. A crew member would reach in through Betsy's side and capture the bull's semen in a plastic bag. The bag of semen was taken over to a box truck parked nearby where it was checked under a microscope and, if it passed that and a few other tests, was quickly processed to separate the sperm. The sperm were then inserted into long, thin metal tubes and stored in a 'cryo' unit in liquid nitrogen.

Joanne asked one of the crew why all this was necessary. Why they couldn't put the bulls with the cows and let nature take its course.

"It's like this, miss," he answered. "Back in the old days that probably worked pretty good. But today the modern ranch needs to operate on a schedule. Bulls and cows together have never heard of a schedule. That's one reason we keep them apart. Then there's another problem. We breed our bulls to be especially excellent specimens. When bulls breed naturally, mistakes sometimes happen. Either they will happen on a poor specimen of a cow and end up crushing the cow, or they will get excited and bungle the job. They have also been known to fall off the cow and break something important, like a leg. Sometimes they are just too big for the cow and they end up crippling her. It's just a mess. We eliminate all of the problems with artificial insemination."

"And take all of the fun out of it?" Joanne thought.

Bill decided to take the long way back to the ranch house. He took the ranch hands to the eastern boundary of the ranch where a crew was riding the fence line and making repairs. The crew welcomed the additional help at spotting breaks in the fence. The ranch hands were just glad to be at a less taxing job. All they had to do was ride along the fence and call a crew member when they saw something that needed attention. Bill informed them that the ranch had well over one hundred miles of fence that needed monitoring. Some of it was wood, but most was barbed wire.

The ranch hands spent almost two full weeks out on the range before they saw the bunkhouse again. When they returned they brought with them many happy memories, and a few strange ones. They also brought a ton of dirt, a few various insects and arachnids and a sunburn or two. A couple of days off at the bunkhouse were more than welcome.

When Joanne checked the schedule in the dining hall, the next item on the agenda simply said 'Wakulla'. There was no time or location posted – just the one word.

Chapter 6

On to Wakulla

Very shortly, several of the ranch hands had gathered around the new 'agenda' posting. All were as confused as Joanne about the meaning of the strange word. Eddie, the cook, came out from the kitchen to see what the commotion was about. Even he did not know what 'Wakulla' meant.

One of the ranch hands spotted Bill Thomas walking by the dining hall and called out to him,

"Bill! Please come in here. We need you."

Bill, fearing the worst, hastened into the dining hall, and was immediately beset by all of the campers wanting to know what the mysterious word on the agenda meant.

Bill, greatly relieved to know the real cause of the alarm, just leaned back against the front door post, smiling.

"Well," he began in his usually laconic style, "Wakulla is the name of a little pretend western town on an Indian reservation in Arizona. It looks like the spittin' image of a western town of a hundred years ago. They have even filmed some movies there. On weekend afternoons in the summer they put on a really nice show: pretend bank robbery, shoot-out, the works. Only problem is, it's about fifty miles from here.

"The ranch hands are going there to see the show this Sunday. We will mount up early tomorrow morning and ride as far as we can. Then we will camp overnight and finish the trip on Sunday. We should get there in time to look the town over and see the show. We will spend the night in Wakulla and have a big campfire. Then we will start back on Monday morning. The chuck wagon will accompany us all the way over and back. Besides providing our meals, it will also serve as a sag wagon."

The shouts from the assembled ranch hands almost drowned out the end of Bill's explanation. But Bill waved them to silence and continued.

"One of the reasons you have been doing so much riding lately was to get you into shape for a long cross-country ride. The ride to and from Wakulla is not going to be any picnic. It is going to be hard work. We here at the Rockin-R hope that you will find the adventure sufficiently enjoyable to make the ride worth it.

"When we rejoin the herd next week, we will help cut out the animals to be sold and then help the crew drive them to the railhead. We will not come back to the bunkhouse until they are on the train and on the way to the slaughter house – in about two weeks.

"After that," Bill concluded, "we will end the summer by rounding up a few horses to be trained for next year. Now, I suggest to go do your wash and pack for a few weeks on the range."

The dining room emptied instantly as the ranch hands headed out to spread the word: Wakulla!

All of the ranch hands were especially busy that day. A few had let laundry duties slip by, knowing that there would always be tomorrow or next week. Now tomorrow and next week had arrived simultaneously and the older ones knew only too well the penalty for getting too smelly.

After supper there was a big campfire scheduled. Desert that night would be s'mores around the fire. Joanne had lagged behind when the others rushed out to the fire pit. Bobbi saved her a seat by the fire, but, when Joanne didn't show up. Bobbi became worried and went looking for her. Bobbi finally found Joanne in her bunk. She appeared to be groaning quietly.

"What's the matter, Jo E.?" Bobbi asked as she climbed up on the bottom rail of the bunk.

"Oh, hi Bobbi," Joanne answered. "I just got a headache during supper and thought I'd better rest a bit before the big ride tomorrow."

"Are you alright?", Bobbi persisted.

"Sure, I'll be fine by tomorrow," Joanne said. "You had better get back to the campfire. You can have my desert tonight." Joanne rolled over with her back toward Bobbi.

Bobbi hesitated for a moment. Then she just shrugged and headed rapidly back to the campfire.

Joanne was fast asleep when the others returned from the campfire. Their loud banter and the noise they made getting ready for bed did not faze her. Joanne had some really weird dreams that night. In the first one she had been stripped naked and bent over, only to feel something probing deeply inside her. The probe evoked both pain and pleasure. By the time the dream was over she woke briefly. Something between her legs was throbbing and she was breathing very heavily. She rolled over and went back to sleep.

The second dream was stranger, yet. It began with a deep throbbing in her lower abdomen. The throbbing was accompanied by heavy breathing and then a pain between her legs. The pain persisted; it almost felt good. She was looking for someone or something. She didn't know just what. Then, just as she found what she was looking for, the pain suddenly became severe and disappeared. She felt greatly relieved. She tossed and turned the rest of the night, but there were no more dreams.

Bill roused the ranch hands just before dawn. Everyone dressed quickly and gathered their supplies for the ride and headed to the corral to saddle up. Joanne was up with the rest, bright eyed and seemingly over her headache of the night before.

The ranch hands set off on their long ride to Wakulla just as the sun was rising over the eastern mountains. Bill advised them that the chuck wagon had already started the journey, as they could only make about twenty-five miles a day fully loaded. Bill was going to pace the ranch hands at a rate of about thirty miles the first day and twenty the second. They rode north and then veered to the west.

Actually, compared to the work they had been doing for the past three weeks, just riding along, singing an occasional song, or, in one small group, telling a few off-color jokes, was a piece of cake. Indeed, when they stopped for lunch, they had caught up with the chuck wagon, and cake was on the desert menu.

As soon as the ranch hands were served lunch from the chuck wagon, Eddie packed up the wagon and took off.

Bobbi rode along with Joanne and kept watching her for any sign her headache had returned, but Joanne gave no hint that she was in distress – until late that afternoon. She began to wobble a bit in the saddle and Bobbi rode up next to her and asked her if everything was okay.

"Yeah, I'm fine," Joanne replied. "Just have a bit of a pain from sitting in the saddle for so long."

"Funny," Bobbi thought, as their horses walked along together, "she has ridden harder than this without any pain … "

About mid afternoon, they came to a gate in the boundary fence. When all the stragglers had caught up, Bill informed them that this was the western boundary of the Rockin'-R ranch. As soon as they passed through the gate they would be in Arizona.

Tim and Rodney dismounted, opened the gate and led their horses through. Then Bill positioned himself by the gate and announced,

"Alright, everyone in single file. Just hand me your signed permission slips as you pass through the gate."

As the ranch hands all hesitated, Bill called out again, "What? Forgot your permission slips? Looks like anybody who doesn't have a permission slip will have to ride back to the ranch and get one."

Joanne was completely confused and baffled. Then she realized that Tim and Rodney were already in Arizona and they had not handed Bill any permission slip. It was all just a gag! She nudged Molly forward and motioned to Bobbi to follow her.

As she got to Bill, she simply said, "I'm not wearing a dress; I don't have a slip with me." As she and Bobbi rode on through the gate.

Bill whispered after her, "Spoil sport." Then he announced to the other ranch hands, "Well, come on, guys, we haven't got all day."

They camped that night on the top of some small hills. They had a clear view of the surrounding country and could even see the dim lights of some of the larger towns far in the distance. Bobbi, who was still watching Joanne rather closely, saw her limping in the chow line. After eating quickly, Joanne went back to her bedroll and settled in for the night, completely ignoring the campfire.

Bobbi went over and sat down next to her. "What's wrong, Jo E." she asked. "Do you want me to get Bill?"

"No!" was the emphatic answer. "Just leave me alone. I'll be fine in the morning." Bobbi backed off and went over to the campfire. She was getting seriously worried about her friend.

Joanne continued to dream that night, but her dreams were not as severe as the night before. In one of them, she was having a conversation with someone. Their mouths weren't moving, but they each clearly understood what the other 'said'. In the other she was searching for something again, something in her past. No matter how hard she searched, she never found what she was looking for. Strangely, she awoke in the morning much more stressed than she had been the previous morning.

Joanne was no longer limping when she rose and appeared as healthy as always. That made Bobbi happier, but she didn't stop worrying. The chuck wagon had left camp before dawn, leaving behind bear claws and coffee for breakfast and sandwiches for lunch. If all went well, the ranch hands would meet the chuck wagon again at Wakulla.

The country was hillier now and their journey would take longer to make the last few miles. It was just after the lunch break and a scant five miles from Wakulla, when Joanne let out an audible groan and slumped forward in her saddle.

Bobbi, who was riding beside her, reached over for Joanne's reins and yelled for Bill. He heard the shout, reined in and looked back. Then he called for everyone to halt and quickly rode back to where Bobbi and Joanne were riding.

"What's the matter?" he asked as he came up to the two. Bobbi just had a confused and worried look on her face. Joanne had recovered somewhat from her last attack. When Bill pressed for an answer to his question, Joanne quietly said, "I need to stop for a few minutes. Can Bobbi stop with me?"

"Of course," Bill said, "We can take a short break here."

"No!" Joanne persisted. "Just Bobbi and I. We will rejoin the ride in a few minutes."

"What?" Bill was perplexed. "No, that is definitely not a good idea."

"Bill, please," Joanne begged. "Female problems." She had seen that ploy used once in an old movie and she hoped it would have the desired effect. It did.

"Oh. Oh!" Bill said, properly intimidated. "Of course! Just a few minutes. And be sure you touch base with me when you get back to the ride." With that, he rode back to the head of the line and told the ranch hands to move on, at a walk.

Joanne and Bobbi waited until the group of boys was almost out of sight. Then Joanne got down from Molly and rummaged around in her saddle bag. She pulled out a panty liner, dropped her jeans and secured the pad securely to the inside of her panties.

"Period?" Bobbi asked. "So soon? Maybe it was all the riding we've been doing ... "

"Yeah, maybe" was all that Joanne could say. She didn't really believe it. The pains she had been feeling in her head and groin were nothing like anything she had ever read about in her mother's nursing books.

Joanne remounted Molly and the two girls rode off at a trot to rejoin the ride.

The ride reached Wakulla about 2:00 PM. The ranch hands were encamped in a small grove at the east end of town opposite the stable. They put their horses in the corral and unsaddled them. Next it was time to care for the horses: rubdown, food and water. After tending to their horses, they had plenty of time to select a place to bed down for the night and set out their gear. Then they were turned loose to browse through the town until the four 'clock show.

"I think I see a general store down the street," Joanne said. "I'm going to see if they have some pain reliever."

"I'll come with you," Bobbi said. She trailed after Joanne.

The general store was almost deserted when Joanne and Bobbie got there. Everyone was gathering outside for the show. Joanne wandered around the store. Bobbi tried to keep her eye on Joanne, but she also kept looking out toward the street.

"Oh, go on out there and watch the show," Joanne said. "I'll be out in a minute."

That was all the encouragement it took. Bobbi made a bee-line for the door.

"Can I help you with something?" John, the proprietor asked from behind the counter.

"Uh, feminine products?" Joanne asked tentatively.

"Far side of the last set of shelves, next to the wall." John muttered.

Joanne made her way behind the shelves. She was out of sight for a few minutes, then John heard a loud groan followed by a thud. He went to investigate and found the young girl lying on the floor, apparently out cold. John was about to panic. He knew nothing of first aid or medicine. He especially knew nothing about 'female problems'. What was he going to do with some sick or injured white kid?

Looking around for anything or anyone that could be of assistance, John chanced to see Nancy Little Dove through the store's front window. He knew that Little Dove was a nurse in the Tucson hospital. He quickly ran outside and tapped her on the shoulder.

"Quick!" he whispered. "Inside! It's an emergency!"

Chapter 7

Puberty Strikes

Little Dove followed John back into the store. Joanne was still lying on the floor. Little Dove immediately knelt down beside the young girl and reached for a pulse. She couldn't find one on either side of the girl's neck. She tried again at her wrists. No pulse. Little Dove looked carefully at the young girl; she appeared to be breathing steadily and easily.

Little Dove was momentarily baffled. From the sound outside, the show was just getting started. She glanced out the window while she was thinking about her options and saw a familiar figure. She suddenly knew just what to do.

"John," she directed, "go outside, find Red Hawk and tell her that I need her help now. In the meantime, I'll take the girl into the back room." When John hesitated a second too long, Little Dove barked out sternly, "Now! John." John practically fled to the door.

Little Dove quickly checked the young girl for possible broken bones and, finding none, picked her up and moved her through the door at the back of the store.

The back room was a storage space for a hodge-podge of leftovers and new stock. There were no windows and only the door to store and another door opposite it to the parking lot. Little Dove maneuvered the young girl and herself through the door and kicked it closed. Then she looked around for some suitable spot to lay her and settled on a pile of empty feed sacks.

While she waited for Red Hawk to appear, Little Dove continued to check the girl for abrasion, contusions, or any other visible injury. She found nothing. Just some dust from the store's floor.

The door to the store suddenly opened and Red Hawk entered the back room. She was the tribe's shaman and an imposing figure. She stood almost six feet tall with red hair and well-tanned skin. Her hair was held in place with a beaded headband. She was wearing a soft buckskin dress, split from shoulder to hem down each side. The dress was held in place by a thin leather belt that also held a knife scabbard. A medicine bag swung easily from her neck.

"What's going on, Dovey? Red Hawk asked.

"I'm not sure," Little Dove answered. "She collapsed in the store and has been out ever since. I can't get a pulse, but she seems to be breathing without any problem. No visible marks or broken bones. That's as far as I've gotten."

"Let's see what I can find," Red Hawk said. She knelt beside the girl, went into a light trance and began moving her hands slowly over the girl's body. In a few seconds, she paused with one hand over the girls head and the other over her groin. Red Hawk came out of her trance and looked, no, stared at the position of her hands. She was remembering a past experience. Then she shook her head as though to dispel some lingering thought.

Red Hawk turned to John, who had returned and was standing in the doorway. "John," Red Hawk ordered, her voice in tome that was not to be disobeyed, "if anyone should ask you about this girl

58

you are to tell them only that she came into the store, looked around briefly, and left to watch the show. You are to say nothing more. Do you understand?" When John had assented, Red Hawk continued in a lighter voice, "Now go find Billy Eagle and tell him to get over here with his Jeep just as fast as that old heap will run."

Dovey had watched this with some awe. She had seen Red Hawk in action before at tribal functions, but it had never been anything like this performance.

"Dovey," Red hawk said calmly, "I may be needing your assistance tonight. Will you help me?"

"Of course, Red Hawk," was Little Dove's immediate reply.

"Then we will wait for Billy to get here." Red Hawk said as she went back into a trance and resumed running her hands over the girl's body.

It was almost ten minutes before the sound of Billy's Jeep was heard outside behind the store. Billy came into the room through the back door and made his way around a few piles of barrels and boxes to where Red Hawk and Little Dove were seated next to the young girl. He took in the scene in a single glance.

"What's going on?" Billy asked.

"It appears that we have a sick camper, Billy" Red Hawk said. "I believe that she has a disease that we haven't seen around here for ten years or so: puberty."

It took Billy a few seconds to register that last comment. Then he just let out a soft whistle. "Are you serious?" he asked. "How is that possible?"

"I don't know, Billy," Red Hawk said. "But I'm going to have to get her to a safe place where I can explore the situation. It may require several days. Will you help me?"

"Of course, Red Hawk," Billy replied. "What do you want me to do?"

"Eventually," Red Hawk thought out loud, "the camp counselor will come looking for this camper. We have to devise some plausible reason to explain her disappearance. I think I know how we can do that with a minimum of fuss and bother.

"Billy, you know Mike down at the stables. Will he cooperate with a little play acting?"

"He will, or he'll spend the night in jail," Billy replied.

"Good," said Red Hawk. "Go up to the stable and get Mike alone. Have him quietly get this girl's horse out of the corral, he will know which one it is. Saddle her and tie her up, out of sight, behind the stable. Then get Dovey's horse ... "

"Stall 4", Dovey interjected.

" ... and Diablo," Red Hawk continued. Saddle Dovey's and throw a couple of blankets on Diablo. Then bring them back down here. And make sure that Mike understands none of this ever happened. Oh, yes," Red Hawk had an afterthought. "Check the girl's horse for tagged shoes."

"Will do!" Billy said and he headed out the back door.

"Now that he is gone," Red Hawk said to Dovey, "let's get you ready for your little role in our drama. I want you to put on this girl's shirt, kerchief and hat. You are just about her size, so they should fit well enough."

Time passed far too slowly waiting for Billy to return. When Billy did get back with the two horses, Red Hawk had him tie them behind his Jeep one on each side. Billy and Little Dove were still not sure exactly what was going on. It was beginning to get dark, and Billy feared that the camp counselor or the other campers would be looking for the missing girl.

"What about the girl's horse, Billy?" Red Hawk asked.

"Tag on the left front foot," Billy said. "Single notch at 11:00."

Red Hawk pulled a knife from a sheath on her waistband and cut a large patch out of one of the feed bags. Then she cut off a length of twine from a handy spool.

"Okay," Red Hawk announced. "We are ready to put on our show. Dovey, It's your turn. I want you to make your way to the stable without being seen. Get on the girl's horse and ride out north toward the 'gap'. It doesn't matter if anyone sees you riding off, just be sure they don't follow you. As soon as you get to the hard ground, stop, and put this patch over the horse's left front foot. Then turn west and head home, keeping as much as possible to the hard ground. We should be there waiting for you."

Little Dove acknowledged her instructions and took off, wearing the girl's clothes. As soon as she was on her way, Billy and Red Hawk carried the young girl out to the Jeep using several feed bags as a stretcher. Red Hawk added a couple more as a covering. The she climbed in the back with the girl and Billy got in the driver's seat.

"Any particular instructions for your chauffer?" he asked.

"Drive directly out to Dovey's cabin," Red Hawk instructed. "Just as though you were making your usual rounds. We'd better get going we don't want to be in the vicinity when they start looking for this girl. Oh, and be sure to take it slow; we have a couple of tag-alongs."

Billy and Little Dove arrived at her cabin almost simultaneously. Red Hawk traded Dovey's horse for the girl's horse and clothes and thanked Dovey for all of her assistance. She reminded Dovey, should anyone ask, that they had ridden out together from Wakulla. Billy tied the girl's horse onto the back of the Jeep and then relocated Diablo in tandem behind her.

Then Billy drove on to Gray Wolf's cabin in the sacred ground. The cabin was located in a small canyon at the southern end of a large butte. Next to the cabin was a sweat lodge and shower. Opposite the cabin, against the far wall of the canyon was a small lean-to and a corral. Red Hawk was using the cabin while Gray Wolf was on the eastern end of the reservation attending a chief's council.

Red Hawk placed both of the horses in the corral and buried the mare's saddle under a pile of blankets and feed bags beneath the overhang. Then she and Billy carried the girl into the cabin and placed her on a bearskin rug next to the fireplace.

Red Hawk thanked Billy for all of his help that evening and cautioned him not to talk about what had gone on.

"I couldn't do that if I wanted to," Billy said. "I still don't understand it all."

Red Hawk suggested that Billy take the long way around back to Wakulla and disappeared inside the cabin.

Chapter 8

A Campers is Missing

When Billy left Red Hawk he patrolled the reservation road for a while and then turned onto the road to Wakulla. The first two miles of the road had now been paved and led directly to the new casino.

Gambling at the old hotel in Wakulla had been so popular that the tribe decided to invest in a brand new casino, halfway between Wakulla and the reservation road. The Casino included two floors of hotel rooms with a full gaming casino on the ground floor. It also had a large parking lot, extensive landscaping and enough lighting to illuminate a small city. Many members of the tribe complained about the light pollution, until the casino's revenue made the issue moot. There was also a tour bus service from the casino to Wakulla for the afternoon shows.

The casino made the hotel in Wakulla just another old relic, but it remained an integral part of the old town with rooms available, slot machines for general use and a card room for special high-stakes poker games.

Billy spent as much time as he dared at the casino. He checked with the casino security staff, watched a few high-priced games and looked over the cars in the parking lot. Eventually, he knew, he had to get back to Wakulla.

Billy parked his Jeep behind his office and began walking his evening rounds. He would go from store to store, ensuring that lights were off and that doors were locked. He had made it past two stores when he heard a call from behind.

"Sheriff!"

Billy turned to see the Rockin'-R counselor approaching form the eastern end of town. He waited until the counselor had caught up with him.

"Good evening," Billy greeted the man. "How can I help you?"

"My name is Bill Thomas," Bill began. "I'm the counselor for the Rockin'-R kids. It seems as though one of our campers is missing."

"Tell me about it," Billy said.

"Well," Bill summarized the situation, "she was last seen in the general store just before the afternoon performance. She didn't show up for supper and she missed bed check. I asked around and none of the other campers has seen her."

"There isn't far she can go and still be in town," Billy suggested. "I am just starting my evening rounds. Why don't we stop by my office so I can get my keys. Maybe she got locked into a store by accident."

Bill agreed and the two walked back to the sheriff's office where Billy got a large metal ring holding the keys to the town's stores. Then they set off toward the western end of town, checking each store or office as they came to it.

At the end of the street they crossed over to the north side of town and stopped at the hotel.

"Hello, Tom," Billy greeted the night manager. "Have you seen any sign of a young female camper hanging around?"

"Now, Sheriff," Tom responded, "you know we don't allow any unaccompanied young people in here."

"Have you chased any out, today?" Billy asked.

"Only a couple of boys," Tom said. "Early this afternoon, before the show. But no girls."

"Tim and Rodney," Bill muttered. "They would! Bet they were in the saloon, too."

Billy thanked Tom for his information. He and Bill Thomas continued checking the stores.

Ken, the barkeeper in the saloon, confirmed that two young boys had indeed been in the saloon before the show. But he affirmed that he had not seen any young girls. While he and Bill Thomas were in the saloon, Billy noted with some satisfaction that Sam Bear-Claw was nursing a bottle at a table in the back.

At the general store, Billy opened the front door and shut off the alarm system so that he and Bill Thomas could investigate more thoroughly the last place Joanne had been seen. They even looked in the back room, but there was no sign of Joanne's presence.

The two continued checking buildings all the way to the stable. There, Billy started to lead Bill Thomas into the trap that Red Hawk had set for him.

"Bill," Billy asked, "have you checked to see whether the girl's horse is still in the corral?"

Bill was stumped at such a question. "Of course," he thought, "the horse had to still be in the corral." But he had to admit that he hadn't checked. He and the sheriff walked over to the corral and took a good look.

"You know," Bill finally said, "I don't see her horse in the corral. It was a little roan mare named, Molly"

"Let's check with Mike," Billy suggested and the two men walked into the stable. "Hey, Mike!" Billy called out.

"Comin," came from the back of the stable where Mike lived most of the time. He hurried toward the front of the stable. As soon as he saw who was waiting for him, he came to an abrupt halt. "What can I do for you, Sheriff?" he asked tentatively.

Billy decided to take the lead, lest Bill ask some embarrassing question. "One of the campers horses is missing from the corral out front. Do you know anything about that?"

Mike looked at Billy a second or two too long, then carefully said, "I didn't saddle up a horse for any of the kids."

Billy looked over at the counselor and asked, "Could this girl have saddled her own horse?"

"Yeah," Bill answered. "She had a super light-weight saddle. She could handle it easily. But, why would she saddle her horse?"

Billy just gave a 'how the hell should I know' shrug. "Is her saddle missing?" he asked Mike.

Mike went back to the area where he had set up some sawhorses to hold the campers' gear and poked around for a minute. "Yeah," he answered, "a saddle and a bridle are missing."

"But her saddlebags and bed roll are still over in the camp area," Bill offered. "What could she have been thinking!?" he exclaimed.

"Looks like she went out for a ride," Billy observed. "You sure you haven't seen anything, Mike?" Billy asked.

Mike glanced at Billy, noted his stern expression and immediately replied, "No, nothing. With all these horses here I have been too busy to notice anything."

"Good old Mike," Billy thought and smiled briefly. Then he turned by to Bill Thomas. "You sure no one at your camp saw her riding off?"

"Yes," Bill answered. "I spent some time canvassing the camp before I came looking for you."

"Well," Billy surmised, "she couldn't leave by the front of the stable without being visible to the people at your camp site or to Mike as he worked in the corral. If she did go riding, she would have to had to leave the stable via the back. Let's take a look."

Billy led the other two to the back of the stable and stopped them just inside the back door. Then Billy turned to Mike and asked, "Anyone take a horse out this evening?"

Mike was beginning to get just a little nervous. "Well, let me think," He said.

"Take your time," Billy told him.

"Yeah," Mike said, looking up. "Red Hawk and Little Dove took their horses out."

"If you were out in the corral," Bill asked, "how could you see them take their horses out and not see Joanne take hers out?"

Mike surprised everyone when he pointed out. "I noticed that their stalls were empty when we

68

walked back here," he said simply. "Their horses were both in their stalls this afternoon."

Billy realized he had been holding his breath and exhaled softly. "Right!" he said. "Tell me, Bill, does the Rockin'-R tag their shoes?"

Bill was a little surprised by the question. He made a mental note not to underestimate this reservation sheriff. "Yes," he answered, "we put a single notch in the left front shoe at eleven o'clock. Why?"

"This area is a mess," Billy pointed to the sand beyond the back door, "and the lighting is poor, but, if she took her horse out of here, there should be some indication of it."

They all looked at the ground outside the stable. Then Billy pointed to a spot near the side of the door. "Look! Over here!"

There in the sand was a clear hoof print with a notch at the proper place. All of the other prints were obviously made by unshod horses.

"That pretty much clinches it," Billy pointed out. "Three horses left the stable. Two were unshod and the third left this print. Looks like that is your answer, Bill."

Bill had paled a bit at the thought of one of his campers alone on the desert at night. Especially one who had been acting strangely of late. He was rather obviously running through a list of possible options open to him.

"Is there any way we can track her?" he asked at last.

"Well," Billy drew it out. "We can probably track her at first light."

69

"Not until morning!" Bill was rapidly heading toward a full blown panic.

"There is very little moon out tonight," Billy observed. "Can't track without light – and artificial light is just no good. Poor shadow definition. If we tried to go out there in the dark we could easily miss a turn or ride over the track we're trying to follow. Much better we wait until morning. Besides, a good tracker will cost you some money. You might want to touch base with the owner of the Rockin'-R before you commit his funds."

Bill had not even thought about Glenn Rogers. What would he say when he found out that one of his campers was missing? A camper who had been placed in Bill's care for an admittedly risky outing.

"Uh, how much money?" Bill asked. Then he quickly added, "Just so I can tell Mr. Rogers."

"Well," Billy replied. "You are in luck. I spotted Sam Bear Claw in the saloon when we were checking buildings. He is by far the finest tracker in this area. I've used him before. He charges $250 per hour for active tracking, with a minimum time of one hour up front."

"The guy in the back, nursing a bottle?" Bill had good observation skills.

"Another reason to wait," Billy suggested. "He'll be cold sober in the morning. I can guarantee that."

"Is there a telephone I can use?" Bill asked.

"Sure, you can use the one in my office," Billy offered.

Billy thanked Mike for all his help. He and Bill Thomas walked back to the sheriff's office. Billy waited outside while Bill told his employer what had happened.

"I may have a job left, if I get all of the campers safely back to the Rockin'-R," Bill said when he came out of the office, "but no guarantee on that." After a brief pause, he asked, "Is there anywhere I can cash a check or get some cash?"

"You have some plastic?" Billy asked.

"Yeah."

"Then I think I can get you a loan at the Hotel," Billy said. "We'll start the track at six AM. Behind the stable. Meet me here at 5:30"

As soon as Bill Thomas left to return to the camp site, Billy went over to the saloon and walked back to the table where Sam was sitting. Billy pulled up a chair next to Sam.

"You awake?" Billy asked. Sam grunted in reply. "Well, I have a track for you at first light. Behind the stable. Be sober!"

Sam gave another grunt and reached for the bottle.

Billy headed back to his office to get some sleep. Tomorrow could be a long day – or not.

Chapter 9

At Track's End

It was still dark when Bill Thomas arrived at the Sheriff's office promptly at 5:30 AM. Billy Eagle was waiting. Billy poured out a cup of coffee into a paper cup for each of them and the two went over to the hotel where the counselor was able to get the money to pay Sam Bear Claw. Then they walked down to the stable where they pitched their cups into the trash and saddled their respective horses. By six o'clock they were mounted and waiting at the back of the stable for Sam.

They didn't have to wait long. Just as the sun was peeking over the eastern mountains, Sam came up behind them so quietly that neither heard him approach.

"So," Sam asked, "what is it I am supposed to track, and for whom?"

"I am looking for one of my campers," Bill said. "We know she rode off from the back of the stable, here, last night. I need to find her as soon as possible."

Sam looked briefly at the designated spot. "Many horses left the stable here," he said. "If I am to track all of them, it will take some time ... "

"No, not all of them," Bill spluttered. "Only the one with a notch in its left front shoe." Bill pointed to the imprint he and Billy had seen the previous night.

"Ah," Sam said, looking back at the ground. "That will not take so long. You have some money for me?"

"Yes," Bill agreed. "$250 for the first hour and a guarantee of payment for as long as it takes to find her." He handed the cash to Sam.

"Then let's go," Sam said. "You two always ride behind me, away from the sun."

Sam turned his horse toward the north and started off. He soon discovered that the trail consisted of only a single horse and increased his speed – slightly. Sam initially hoped that he could stretch this track into several hours. But he soon noticed that Billy was tracking along with him. Unfortunately, for Sam, Billy was an excellent tracker and would keep him honest.

The three rode slightly east of north for just over thirty minutes before the sand gave way to harder ground. The 'gap' was still ahead of them and hills were burgeoning on both sides of it. Almost immediately they were on the stonier ground of the hills. Sam stopped and turned back to the others.

"Tracking over hard ground is trickier," he explained. "Even shoes leave very few marks. And the marks may be farther apart. I have no way of knowing where she went from here: maybe east, maybe west, maybe through the gap."

"You don't mean you're quitting here, do you?" Billy asked.

"No," Sam stated, " but it will take some time to check out each of the possibilities. You two rest here. I will pick up the trail and come back for you. I can travel faster alone."

With that, Sam turned his horse to the east and rode off, carefully scanning the ground as he went.

Billy and Bill Thomas dismounted and found a suitable rock for a seat. Each kept his thoughts to himself. Neither one had anything to share at the moment.

In twenty minutes, Sam returned only to report that he had found no trace of the notched shoe. In fact, he reported, he had seen no sign of any shod horse. He then turned to the north and rode up through the 'gap'.

This time it took some thirty minutes for Sam to return. He again reported that he had seen no sign of a shod horse. Bill had to admit that Joanne was a remarkable young girl, but even he could not envision a way in which she could have removed her horse's shoes.

"So far, so good," Billy thought, almost convinced that Red Hawk's plan was going to work.

"I know she didn't back-track," Sam said. "There's only one option left. We all might as well go on together. Ride behind me and try to stay on the hard ground."

Sam waited while the others mounted then started off toward the west. As before, he rode slowly, carefully watching the ground for any sign of the girl's horse. As soon as the softer sand encroached on the hard ground, Billy, who was also tracking at his best, realized he had a problem. He had definitely seen two horseshoe imprints. No notches, but damning anyway. He knew that Sam had seen them, but Sam had not yet announced his find. Suddenly, Billy had a scathingly brilliant idea.

74

"Sam," Billy called out, "I just saw a couple of shoe prints in the sand. Did you miss those?"

"I didn't miss them, Sheriff," Sam answered curtly. "But they could have come from any shod horse. I have seen no firm evidence that the girl's horse came this way."

"Bingo!" Billy thought. Then he had second thoughts. Sam had said 'firm' evidence. That meant that he had seen something.

Indeed, Sam had noticed something, which was the reason that he was considered the best tracker in the state. The overnight wind about the hills had wreaked havoc with the remaining tracks, but Sam was almost positive that he had seen no trace of a left front foot shoe in the track he was following.

But the track had not been consistent. The rider had kept straying from the sand to the hard ground and back again. Perhaps the rider had been out here at night and could not see clearly. Perhaps the rider was drunk. Perhaps that missing left front shoe print was just a coincidence. But perhaps, just perhaps, that left front shoe had been covered to hide the notch.

Sam stopped suddenly, causing Billy and Bill Thomas to quickly rein in their horses. "Stay put," Sam ordered the other two. He turned and rode briefly back along their trail, studying the ground. When he was satisfied, Sam rode to the head of the line and continued his track.

The new information Sam had obtained brought forth more thoughts. Sam liked Sheriff Billy. And for some reason, Sheriff Billy acted like he didn't want the girl found. Sam also knew that the next cabin up the line belonged to Little Dove. Sam also liked Little Dove. She had ministered to Sam's medical needs for several years at no charge.

At this point, Sam could either prove that the girl's horse likely came this way, or likely didn't come this way. Sam needed still more information, so he pressed on.

In another twenty minutes of slow patient riding the group came up to Little Dove's cabin. It was time for push to meet shove. Sam spent several minutes studying the ground in front of the house.

"Sheriff," Sam asked, "any way I can get a look at Little Dove's pony?"

"I'll check," Billy said. He dismounted, walked up to the door and knocked. When Little Dove answered the door, Billy explained that they were out on a track and asked about Sam checking her pony. Little Dove instantly agreed and Billy signaled her assent to Sam.

Sam dismounted and walked over to the corral. One look at the ground in the corral and Sam didn't have to go any further. Little Dove's pony was not shod. Sam walked back to his horse. He still wanted more time to think. He looked over to Little Dove standing in her doorway and asked, "Little Dove, can we water our horses?" She nodded.

When his horse had sufficient water, Sam handed the reins to Billy and walked back to the tracks in front of the cabin. The tracks were a mess. The tire marks from Billy's old jeep were obvious. Billy's boot heels were also obvious. He had wandered around a bit. There were prints from Little Dove's pony and from a larger unshod horse. Looked like they came from Wakulla shortly after Billy did. Perhaps they all came together. Then Billy drove off to the west and the larger horse followed behind him.

Sam made up his mind. He walked back to Billy, retrieved his horse and mounted. Then he turned to Bill Thomas.

"Mr. Thomas," Sam said slowly, carefully phrasing his words, "I am afraid I have no idea where the girl and her horse are. I tracked them to the hard ground by the gap, but I can't go any farther.

"I am satisfied that she did not ride to the east or to the west and she did not back track to Wakulla. The only remaining option is that she rode up into the gap, maybe across the mountains. The ground up there is too stony and hard to track even a shod horse, so I can't prove that is what she did. I know the Sheriff has been tracking with me and I am sure he will concur with that. I am afraid that we are at the end of the track.

"Since I could not complete the track I will not ask for any more money than that which you paid for the first hour. Perhaps you will be able to find someone who can do a better job for you than I did."

With that final statement, Sam Bear Claw turned his horse and rode off toward Wakulla.

Billy and Bill Thomas just stood there and watched Sam ride off. Little Dove called out to them, "You fellas look a bit trail weary. Would you like to come in for a cup of coffee?"

Bill Thomas begged off. "Sheriff," he asked, "can I use your phone again? I've got to tell Mr. Rogers about this. Then, if I still have a job, I have to rejoin the rest of the campers and get them back to the Rockin'-R before something else happens."

"Thanks for the offer, Dovey," Billy announced as he mounted his horse, "but it looks like we have to go."

The two rode off toward Wakulla following in Sam's dust.

When they got back to town, Billy and Bill Thomas left their horses at the stable and walked to Billy's office.

Bill's call was relatively brief, but not so sweet. Mr. Rogers had held off notifying Mary Gauss of her daughter's disappearance based on Bill's assurance that she would be found. Now Bill had to admit that she was not only missing, but that he had only the vaguest idea where she had gone. And worse, he had no way of finding her. Bill's only instructions for the moment were to get the remaining campers back to the Rockin'-R before any more of them wandered away or got themselves lost.

Bill hastened to thank Sheriff Billy for all of his help. Then he ran back to the corral, mounted his horse and headed out of town to the east. He didn't take the time to tell Billy what other plans Mr. Rogers had in mind.

As for Billy, he just heaved a sigh of relief. Apparently Red Hawk's plan was going to work, after all. He had no idea that the roof was about to fall in.

Chapter 10

A New Breed

As soon as Billy had left Gray Wolf's cabin, Red Hawk began working on the young girl. She removed the girl's clothing so that she could make a complete physical examination of her body. There were no obvious injuries, no broken bones. Yet the girl had been in pain. It had to be internal.

Red Hawk stretched the girl out on the bearskin and checked for a pulse. Like Little Dove before her, Red Hawk could not get a pulse in any of the usual places. She verified that the girl was still breathing – easily and deeply, as though she were simply asleep.

Red Hawk sat back to ponder the situation. Night had fallen. The cabin was dark and was getting chilly. Red Hawk moved over to the fire place and started a small fire. The cabin was soon warm and illuminated by a soft yellow glow. They would now be more comfortable, but she had not solved the original problem.

It was time to give in and do what she knew was necessary – no matter how ridiculous it was. She knelt beside the girl and slowly went into a trance. She moved her hands over the girl's head to help her focus. She had never probed an unconscious mind before. Red Hawk thought back ten years. Back to the time she had assisted Ari-Ana with the Elder children.

The Elders were an ancient alien race who had accidentally been stranded on Earth over a thousand years ago. They had lived hidden away in the butte next to Gray Wolf's cabin for all that time. Then one of their number was accidentally killed by a truck driver, who took her child and raised it as a human. Ten years later the child came to the attention of Dr. Joanne Archer, who was working in Tucson at the time. Fascinated by the child and her obviously alien attributes, Dr. Archer became the shaman, Red Hawk, so that she could continue to interact with the child. In doing so, she was welcomed into the Elder community. Part of that interaction involved helping Elder children through puberty to adulthood. Her teacher in this endeavor was Ari-Ana, an Elder councilor.

Now Red Hawk wondered if she was faced with a similar situation. Could this little girl, who outwardly appeared to be entirely human, actually be part Elder? The Elders were entirely hairless. This girl had hair in all the right human places. Elders' eyes consisted of a single large lens, which made them appear completely black; this girl's eyes consisted of a smaller lens surrounded by a colored iris and white sclera. She was an inch or two taller than the average Elder. Elder palms and soles had retractable scales; her palms and soles were smooth.

Yet, she did not have an externally detectable pulse; her major blood vessels were all deeply internal, with only the tiniest capillaries reaching to the surface of the limbs. Elders had neither intestines nor anus. Red Hawk had to look; she spread the girls legs. She had a urethra, a vagina, and, curiously, an anus. Outwardly, the girl appeared to be totally human. Then it began to dawn on Red Hawk. She was some sort of a new breed. A blend of Elder and Human. However that may have been achieved.

That realization made the diagnosis of the child's problem academic. She was indeed going through puberty! Red Hawk turned her attention back to the child. She did her best to remember all the techniques she had been taught for dealing with Elder children and went to work. First the brain needed attention. An Elder child's brain was opening up new pathways and new sections of the brain. Unless it was controlled, it would cause massive headaches and could result in death.

Red Hawk went into a deep trance and probed the child's brain. There were some familiar pathways being developed. She was able to free up a snarl or two. But the greatest benefit lay in her ability to calm the mind. It was something akin to working the knots out of a cramping muscle. As soon as the brain could be induced to relax, the pain would recede and the healing could commence.

The same was true with the groin. An Elder's penis would develop about this time. But the juvenile penis was encased in a sac or pouch. The sac had to rupture in just the right place to allow the penis the necessary freedom of movement to penetrate the vagina. Again the best treatment involved relaxing the muscles until just the right moment.

The child was beginning to moan and move as though she were having a bad dream. Red Hawk had no way of knowing what the dream was about. The best she could do was to place the child into a deep sleep. That would solve both of their problems for several hours.

Red Hawk got up, took her dress off and carefully folded it. Then she went outside and availed herself of Gray Wolf's toilet and shower.

Completely refreshed, she returned to the cabin and bedded down next to the bear rug for the night.

The next morning Red Hawk kept the fire going long enough to brew a small pot of coffee. Coffee was the one vice she allowed herself on the reservation. When it was ready, she put out the fire, poured a cup and opened the door to let in some fresh air. She went outside and sat down on Gray Wolf's porch and sipped her coffee. When the coffee was cold, it was time to get back to work.

When Red Hawk again examined the girl, she discovered that tension had built up over night. She relieved the new tension and soon had the girl resting easily. This would be her job over the next day or so: monitor the penis and relieve tension in the brain.

Red Hawk began to worry a bit about the penis. The girl's vagina was not as large as that of the average Elder. Fitting two penes into her vagina at the same time was going to be a challenge. But, that would be the child's problem at some later date.

Red Hawk was still trying to put the pieces of this puzzle together. Obviously, this child was the product of an Elder/Human connection. An Elder was both male and female. But in this case the human almost had to be a female. There was something gnawing at the back of her brain. But Red Hawk couldn't quite bring it out into the open. She would have to wait.

And wait she did. All that day and most of the next. Finally, all of the changes to the girl's brain had worked themselves out. The tension was greatly diminished. Red Hawk was in a peyote enhanced trance looking at what had transpired. The girl had a brand new lobe in her brain. One that Red Hawk had never seen before in an Elder. She examined it as thoroughly as possible under the circumstances. She wished that Ari-Ana were still here to guide her. Eventually she had to admit defeat and give up on the brain.

The penis was her next target. It had tripled in length and was ready to burst out of its sac. If everything worked as it was supposed to, the girl's pelvic muscles would do the job. Sometimes, they just needed a little prodding to get started or to apply the proper force in the proper direction. Red Hawk just knelt beside the girl and observed.

Two hours later it was all over. Red Hawk had to give the penis an assist, but it neatly slipped into the side of the vagina. At this point it was critical that the girl be able to rest. The amount of energy required by the puberty process was significant. Besides, the girl had not had nourishment since the process had started. When she woke, she would be ravenous.

Red Hawk realized she also had not eaten. She found some jerky in Gray Wolf's larder, It made her stomach feel better. Then she put some wood on the fire and settled in for a good night's rest.

In the morning, Red Hawk woke instantly at the girl's first stirring. When the girl showed signs of serious consciousness, Red Hawk greeted her with a cheery,

"Good morning!"

"Huh?" was her first utterance. It was quickly followed by: "Where am I?", "Who are You?" and "Why am I naked?"

"Let's go get cleaned up," Red Hawk said, "Then I'll tell you all about it."

Red Hawk led the girl outside to the toilet and shower. The girl took to both of them as though she had been there before. They dried off with a communal towel and went back inside the cabin. Red Hawk left the door open as was her custom.

Red Hawk fixed eggs and biscuits and coffee for breakfast. Since Gray Wolf only had one chair for use at the table, she suggested eating on the front porch. They ate in silence. When they had downed the last of the food and coffee, Red Hawk broke the ice.

"My name is Red Hawk," she said. "I am the tribal shaman. Now if you will answer a question for me, maybe we can clear everything up. Until now I have been thinking of you only as 'the girl'. Tell me, what's your name?"

"My name is 'Joanne', the girl said.

"Well, Joanne," Red Hawk said with some astonishment, "My name also happens to be 'Joanne'. Off the reservation I am known as Dr. Joanne Archer. I work at the Winton hospital."

"Doctor?"

"Psychology." Red Hawk answered. "As to your other questions, you are sitting on the front stoop of Gray Wolf's cabin just west of Wakulla. Oh, yes, Gray Wolf is the retiring shaman of the tribe. He is away right now Sometime very soon I will be his permanent replacement.

"You and I were naked because neither of us had any pajamas."

"Why am I here? The last thing I can remember is riding into Wakulla."

"That is going to take some explaining," Red Hawk stalled. "Do you know who your father was?"

"I don't remember him," Joanne said somewhat wistfully. "My mother never talked about him."

"Just who was your mother?" Red Hawk suspiciously.

"Mary Gauss", Joanne replied.

"Gauss ... Gauss," Red Hawk muttered. "Where did I hear that name?" Suddenly it came to her like a bolt out of the blue. It all fit! Enela had arrived late on the morning of the last day. She had been followed by an outraged Jonas Gauss. Enela and Mary ... Joanne was Enela's daughter! Red Hawk was staring at Joanne.

"What's wrong?" Joanne asked. "Do you know my mother?" Then she had a wonderful thought, "Do you know my father!?" she asked impulsively.

"I have never met your mother," Red Hawk said, "but, I know your 'father' very well. Oh, Joanne," she exclaimed, "I have so much to tell you ..."

Red Hawk spent the rest of the morning and most of the afternoon telling Joanne all about the Elders; about Enela, her 'father'; about her own unique physiology; about the source of her mother's money; about the events of the Elders' last day on Earth; and about the last few days. The story was frequently interrupted by tears, by smiles, and by hugs.

By the time Red Hawk was finished, the day had almost ended. She suggested that some time in the sweat lodge might be good for both of them. Joanne was curiously fascinated by the idea.

Joanne helped Red Hawk with the preparations and very shortly the lodge fire was stoked and ready. The two entered the lodge and, as soon as Joanne was seated on a log bench, Red Hawk closed the door flap and put the first of many pots of water on the hot stones.

Joanne held up remarkably well under the heat. When she could handle no more, Red Hawk helped her out and under an icy shower. Joanne was completely refreshed.

Red Hawk and Joanne raided Gray Wolf's pantry for supper. Then Red Hawk brought up Joanne's final test.

"Do you fell well enough to go back to the ranch?" she asked.

"I guess so," Joanne admitted. Then she had another thought. "The other kids have already left Wakulla, haven't they?"

"Yes, I suppose so," Red Hawk replied. "You'll have to ride back alone. Or, we could always call your mother and have her pick you up in Wakulla."

"Ugh, no way," was Joanne's considered opinion. "I can remember some of the route. Can you get me started?"

"Yes," Red Hawk answered. "I'll take you part of the way around Wakulla, and give you instructions on how to get to New Mexico. You realize you will have to spend one night alone on the trail?"

"No problem!"

"Alright, then, let's get some sleep."

Red Hawk woke Joanne well before dawn the next morning. She held a lantern while Joanne saddled her horse. Joanne did not have her bedroll, so Red Hawk gave her an extra blanket and a skin of water, and another skin of jerky. Red Hawk threw a couple of blankets on Diablo and they were off. Red Hawk also put the burlap back on Molly's left front foot, just as a precaution. She had no idea what had been transpiring back in Wakulla.

The two rode out of the canyon and headed due east. Red Hawk followed the same path in reverse that Sam and Billy had followed only a few days earlier. When they got to the vicinity of the 'gap', Red Hawk stopped and took the burlap off of Molly's foot and briefed Joanne on her cover story. She warned Joanne, never to tell anyone but her mother what had actually happened.

From 'the gap' they continued to the east for a mile or so, then turned south east. When they were due east of Wakulla, Red Hawk told Joanne that she was on her own. It was getting light and she would be able to navigate by watching the sun. She snapped a long spine off a nearby cactus and told Joanne that if she put the spine in the center of her watch dial, and aligned the shadow to the current time, the six would point approximately to the south. No, it wasn't completely accurate, but it was close enough, if you didn't happen to have a compass.

She also pointed out Mt Graham in the distance and told Joanne to ride around the south side of the mountain and then head southeast when she got back to flat land.

"You'll eventually hit the fence of the Rockin'-R", Red Hawk said. "If the fence is aligned east-west, ride along the fence to the west until it turns south. If the fence is aligned north-south, ride north along the fence. Once you're inside the gate, just follow the fence until you can see the top of the barn. Good luck."

Joanne thanked Red Hawk for all of her help, turned her horse to the southeast and rode off to a very uncertain future.

Red Hawk waited for a bit, watching Joanne. Something was bothering her. Something just wasn't quite right. She couldn't put her finger on it, but it was there. It persisted hovering just out of consciousness.

Red Hawk finally gave up and turned Diablo toward Wakulla. Then she turned back toward Joanne, receding in the distance. She made up her mind. She reached out to her spirit guide, Koya, the great red falcon.

Koya was eyeing his breakfast at the moment. Joanne waited while the hawk dove onto his prey, grabbed it in his strong talons and soared back up to his perch on the top of the butte. A few more minutes and breakfast was over.

"Koya," Red Hawk called out, "I have need of your services."

"What is it?" Koya asked in return. "And what do I get?"

"A leisurely flight, perhaps some excitement, and new, richer feeding grounds," Red Hawk offered.

"I'll consider it," Koya replied.

"I need you to follow a young rider," Red Hawk told the falcon. "See that she safely leaves the reservation." Red Hawk also sent an image of Joanne. She hoped that the image was sufficiently accurate; hawks had excellent eyesight and could be so picky.

"Done," said Koya. Moments later the hawk was looping lazily overhead on the updrafts from the rapidly heating desert.

Red Hawk's concerns seemed to evaporate. She watched a few minutes more then turned Diablo west toward Wakulla.

Chapter 11

The FBI is Here

Billy had breathed a sigh of relief when Bill Thomas took off for the Rockin'-R. He was certain that his troubles were over. Red Hawk had the little girl in tow; she was in good hands. Everything would soon be back to normal. Billy settled back into his usual routine.

The next morning, Billy had just finished breakfast and was in the back of his office cleaning the dish, when he heard the front door open abruptly.

"Sheriff?" came a brusque call from the front office.

Billy didn't recognize the voice. He put the dish down and walked out to meet his visitor.

"Can I help you?", he asked as he eyeballed the gentleman who was standing in the office. He was dressed in a dark blue suit, but it wasn't well pressed at the moment. He was wearing black oxfords that were still relatively clean.

"I am Special Agent Steve Walker," the man said, flashing what appeared to be an FBI Identification card and badge. "Where can I park my helicopter?"

Billy had started to extend his hand in welcome. On hearing the agent's last word, he stopped instinctively and did a double take.

"Did you say, 'helicopter'? Billy asked.

"Yes," the agent answered. "It should arrive in about 15 minutes. Now, where can I park it? I have to notify the pilot."

Billy was still recoiling from the initial shock. He desperately tried to clear his mind long enough to generate a clear thought. "What kind of helicopter is it?" Billy stammered. "I mean, how big is it?"

"Not so large," Walker said. "Needs about a minimum forty foot clearance," He was hefting a small radio in his hand. He was also becoming impatient.

"Well," Billy stalled while he gave the matter some thought. "We don't get too many folk dropping in by helicopter. I'm afraid we don't have a designated helipad ... "

"Sheriff! ETA is now 10 minutes." Walker announced.

Billy looked at him and noticed the ear bud in his right ear. "Okay," he said, "For now just park it south of the campground on the east end of town. Far enough off that it won't scare any of the horses in the corral."

Walker immediately gave the appropriate instructions over his radio.

"Now, Special Agent Walker," Billy demanded as he sat down at his desk. "You have just nine minutes to tell me what the hell you are doing before I pull that landing permission right out from under you."

"You didn't get our message?" Walker asked, somewhat amazed.

"No," Billy said cautiously, "no message."

"I am sorry," Walker admitted. "I thought you knew."

"Knew what?!" Billy was getting frustrated by Walker's tactics. And Billy was dangerous when he was frustrated.

"I'm from the Tucson office," Walker explained. "Our office was notified yesterday that a young girl was missing from Wakulla and presumed kidnapped. We were also informed that your resources to locate her had been exhausted. We were asked to lend assistance. I take it that you didn't make the request … "

"No, I didn't" Billy stated flatly. "I was aware that one of the Rockin'-R campers was missing. And I did arrange for our best tracker to locate her. He tracked her out of town into the hills up north before he lost the trail. He and I presumed that she had ridden through the 'gap' onto the Apache reservation. At that point she was off my reservation and out of my jurisdiction. The Rockin'-R representative left town yesterday. He did not divulge what further action they were going to take, if any."

"Again, I am sorry for the sudden entrance," Walker said convincingly. "I was under the impression that you had been briefed on what is going on."

"What exactly is going on?" Billy asked only somewhat mollified.

"We are going to do an electronic search of the surrounding area by air," Walker explained. "We have a specially modified AH-6 helicopter about to land. If you will assist us in devising a logical search plan, we should be able to locate the girl within 24 hours."

"If you don't mind my asking," Billy said, "Just what kind of electronics are you talking about?"

"No, not at all," Walker said. "We have color television, forward-looking infra-red, side-looking radar and a sonic listening device available in the helicopter. With the appropriate recording devices."

Billy just let out a low whistle.

"They're coming in now," Walker announced. "Want to go take a look?"

Billy readily nodded and the two men walked out to the east end of town where the little helicopter was setting down in a great storm of blowing sand. Billy gave the machine a good going over. It was painted black. There was room for the pilot and an observer in a small bubble-like front compartment. Special displays for the observer were mounted in front of the right seat. In the back compartment was another seat for the equipment operator among an assortment of screens and displays. With the door closed, that compartment was completely enclosed with no windows.

"Very impressive," Billy announced following his inspection.

"We can move out quickly or linger slowly over a target area for two hours," Walker offered. "The helicopter can be almost silent when it is hovering or moving slowly.

Walker introduced Billy to the two crew members, Kevin Meyers, the pilot and Dan Wilson, the systems tech. Kevin was a younger man, wearing a tight fitting flight suit, with blond hair and very dark glasses. Dan was older, with dark hair and a bit on the heavier side. He was wearing a plain cotton shirt and blue jeans. After they shook hands, Walker was ready to get down to business.

"Now, I'd like to get our search area defined and get started. We can operate in daylight or at night and I don't want to waste any time."

Billy and Walked headed back to the sheriff's office. One the way Billy asked, "Where are you going to refuel? We don't have any filling stations in Wakulla."

"We have made arrangements in Winton," Walker explained.

Back at the office, Billy pulled out several maps of the local area. He pointed out the 'gap', where Sam lost the track, and the location of the Apache reservation. He also showed Walker the reservation highway to the west and the main housing area to the east,

"That area west of the highway around the two large buttes," Billy explained in a very serious tone, " is considered sacred ground by this tribe. It is a registered no-fly zone. I fully expect you to recognize and honor that limit. Besides," he added, "there is absolutely no evidence to suggest that the little girl was ever anywhere near that area."

"And if I don't?" Walker asked.

"Then I will personally see just how bullet-proof that little helicopter is," Billy said menacingly. He indicated the .30-caliber carbine hanging on the wall of his office. "And your permission to fly anywhere over this reservation will evaporate instantly," Billy added.

"You can't do that," Walker bluffed.

"Don't try me," Billy just stated flatly. "Now, let's get your search pattern worked out."

The two worked with the maps for about thirty minutes. In the end it was agreed that the helicopter would first make a complete sweep of the 'gap' and the surrounding area. If nothing was found there, the helicopter would fly a regular search pattern between the highway and the housing area. Breaks for fuel and crew rest would be taken as needed.

Walker took a copy of the map and started out the door.

"Just a minute," Billy called after him. Walker stopped and turned back.

"What frequency does that radio use," Billy asked, indicating the handset that Walker was carrying. Walker told him, with a quizzical expression.

"Come here", Billy suggested and escorted Walker into his back room. There on a table next to the wall was a rather sophisticated wireless setup. Billy adjusted the frequency. "Let's give it a try," he said.

Walker pressed the transmit button and said, "Testing." The word came clearly out of Billy's speaker.

"Answering," Billy said into his microphone. Walker slightly winced as the word came through his ear bud.

"I use this to keep track of my deputies and monitor things around the reservation." Billy explained. "I also monitor CB Channel 13. Most people shy away from anything numbered '13'.

"While you are searching the reservation," Billy continued, "I will be monitoring this frequency. If it goes dead for any length of time, or I hear a scrambler on the frequency, my trigger finger is going to get mighty itchy. Do you get my drift?"

"This isn't the wild west, Sheriff," Walker said.

"Don't bet on it," Billy answered him. "Just how wild it gets will depend on you. We're both after the same thing – to find that girl, if she is anywhere around here. Let's just cooperate, okay?"

"Okay," Walker said, somewhat grudgingly, and headed out the door. Billy soon heard the helicopter's engine racing as it took off.

Chapter 12

Success?

Kevin and Dan were looking forward to a short assignment when they took off. If the girl was anywhere on the reservation they were certain they could locate her within a matter of hours. Dan was sitting in front with Kevin. He wanted to get some idea of the lay of the land. The interior of the helicopter was somewhat noisy, so the two were in communication via internal radio. If necessary, either could switch to the frequency that Walker was using to monitor the mission.

Kevin took the helicopter north from Wakulla toward the 'gap'. Dan powered up his equipment and fine-tuned everything. He planned to rely on the TV camera and use his other tools only when the situation required them.

They reached the 'gap' in a few minutes and Kevin powered back into surveillance mode. He took the helicopter as close to the ground as he dared.

"Hover!" Dan said sharply. He directed his camera toward the ground just in front. "Multiple hoof prints," he told Kevin. "Just as the sheriff described. Let's take it slow here."

Kevin nudged the Helicopter forward and carefully watched the terrain ahead and to either side. Dan focused his camera on the ground below.

"Cave, left" Kevin announced. Dan immediately swung the camera to the left and used it to probe the cave. "Shallow and empty," he said. "No sign of occupancy. Besides, their tracker would most likely have checked anything within a fifteen minute ride from the desert."

So the flight went. They found a few other caves. Some were larger and deeper. One contained a sleeping bear, who was angry at having been disturbed. None of the caves showed any sign of human occupancy. Every time they came to a patch of sand, Dan studied it carefully for any sign of hoof prints. There weren't any past the point at which the tracker would have turned around.

"What do you think about the lack of hoof prints?" Kevin asked after the first hour of searching.

"Personally, I think we are on a wild goose chase up here," Dan admitted. "But, professionally, we can't rule anything out at this early date. We'll keep on with the search."

The most intriguing prospect they found was what appeared to be an old mine. Kevin landed the helicopter near the entrance and the two got out to investigate. They brought hard-hats and lanterns from the helicopter and carefully made their way into the mine. There was no sign of hoof prints near the entrance. No sign of human habitation inside. That is, until Dan pointed to an object laying on the ground some twenty feet inside. Kevin looked. It appeared to be a used condom.

That raised a serious question: a couple of teenagers making out, or some dude who had just raped a ten-year-old girl? They continued probing the cave. About thirty feet from the entrance they came to a dead end. The ceiling had collapsed, blocking any farther investigation. They returned to the helicopter, stowed their equipment and reported their find to Walker.

Another hour's fruitless searching and it was time to fly to Winton for fuel. Then they returned to the 'gap' and resumed their flight plan. The remainder of the morning and the afternoon was just as fruitless. Dan did, however, form a definite hypothesis about the 'gap'.

That evening, Kevin and Dan were relieved by another crew who would be flying the night-time reconnaissance over the reservation. Dan and Walker met for supper at a hotel in Winton.

"That girl definitely did not go up into the 'gap'," Dan insisted. "I examined every patch of sand we came across. There were no hoof prints or boot prints anywhere. The sand was perfectly smooth. Not even any evidence of prints being rubbed out."

"Does Kevin agree?" Walker asked.

"Kevin was too busy keeping us level and away from any outcroppings," Dan answered, "to spend as much time as I did watching the camera input. I would guess that there is maybe one chance in a thousand that the girl could have ridden through the 'gap' without leaving any trace."

"What about the track?" Walker persisted.

"Oh I don't dispute that the girl, or someone riding the girl's horse," Dan explained, "rode up to the 'gap', but she, or he, did not ride through the 'gap'. Oh, I'm certainly not suggesting that this is all some fantastic plot. But, I would concentrate on the horse. A horse is, after all, much harder to conceal that a little girl. Find the horse and you will either find the girl or be close to doing so."

99

"I think," Walker mused, "that tomorrow we will concentrate on the ground as well as the air. The helicopter will keep them from moving the horse around while we emphasize a ground search of the entire reservation."

Indeed, the next morning, three teams of FBI agents spread out across the reservation. Two teams began at 6:00 AM in the eastern end of the reservation, going from house to house. The chief was somewhat unhappy, when he was awakened at seven o'clock by a knock on the door. The teams checked houses, sheds, barns. They moved quickly, only stopping to chat if a horse was found that happened to match the girls'.

The other team moved quickly through Wakulla and the surrounding area. They checked at each of the cabins, the casino, and each of the stores in town, ending at the stable.

After all of this, they found – nothing. No horse, no girl.

That evening, Walker was not a happy camper. He was especially disappointed in Dan's previous information, and told him as much. He assigned Kevin and Dan back into the helicopter for night surveillance and essentially told them that they had better come up with something.

Walker also thought about possibilities for the morning. He kept thinking about Billy's injunction to avoid the 'sacred ground west of the highway.

First, there was the highway. Either the girl or the horse, or both could have escaped the reservation via the highway. What if the girl had ridden to the highway, turned her horse loose and thumbed a ride? Billy and the tracker and the people who lived along the northern hill line all swore that she had not ridden that way. Such a grand conspiracy was just not plausible.

Second, she could be in hiding somewhere on the sacred ground. Suppose she didn't ride there but was taken there? In the sheriff's jeep? That would only require a conspiracy of one. But, then what happened to the horse? That was why Dan had said, 'find the horse'.

"Well," Walker thought, "that damn horse is nowhere on this reservation where we have searched. So it is either entirely off the reservation, or it is across the highway." Walker almost grabbed his radio and ordered the helicopter to head for the sacred ground. But he remembered the sheriff's warning. No, tomorrow would be soon enough. He had the helicopter covering the central area tonight.

Kevin and Dan had flown all night. They had covered the reservation from one end to the other, over and over again. They had only left the reservation for a random fuel stop. After which they had immediately returned. Dan had spent the night in the closed compartment. He was cramped and somewhat bleary eyed. On their last fuel stop before morning, he had moved up front with Kevin. It would be dawn soon and he could revert completely to the TV camera.

At the moment they were flying slowly in the northeastern quadrant of the reservation. Dan's attention was directed to the FLIR screen.

Suddenly, Dan called out, "Hover!"

Kevin stopped the helicopter on a dime. "What is it?" he asked.

"Rider approaching from the east on horseback
," Dan responded. "Small of stature. Could be the
girl."

Kevin switched on the helicopter's spotlight and
lit up the rider. Then he keyed the speaker system
and announced, "Rider, halt your horse. This is the
FBI."

The helicopter's microphone picked up the
deep, threatening response, "And I am Gray Wolf,
Shaman of this tribe! Turn off your light! You are
blinding my horse!"

The rider immediately swung his horse around,
away from the light, but he did not ride off.

By now, Dan had a close-up of the rider on the
TV screen. He immediately called out to Kevin,
"He's right, switch off the light!"

Kevin did not hesitate to do what he was told.
"Sorry," he said over the speaker, "Our mistake.
Please continue on your way."

Kevin banked the helicopter to the southeast.
"That was downright embarrassing," he admitted.

They continued the surveillance for another
twenty minutes. The sun was about to peak out over
the mountains when another rider came into view on
the FLIR.

"This is our lucky day," Dan observed. "But
let's be a little more careful this time." He switched
on the TV camera and adjusted for dim light. It
wasn't perfect, but he had a reasonably good picture.
"Kevin, this could be it!" Dan exulted. "Move over
and hover right in front of the rider, then point the
light down and turn it on."

Joanne had heard the helicopter buzzing around in the sky, but she could not locate it in the dim pre-dawn light. Then, suddenly, it was right in front of her. She thought about turning Molly and making a run for it, but that plan wouldn't hold up. She knew she could not out run a helicopter.

The helicopter's light came on, making the desert as bright as daylight. She was immediately thankful it wasn't aimed directly at her. A voice boomed out, "Halt your horse and dismount."

Joanne was truly afraid, but she saw no way out. She was about to obey the voice when all hell suddenly broke loose.

With a shrill cry, Koya came streaking out of the sky and dove right through a small open window on the side of the helicopter. The front cockpit was cramped enough with just Dan and Kevin sitting there. Add a mad falcon to the mix and chaos was the immediate result. Dan just put his arms and hands up to protect his face. But Kevin had to fly the helicopter, and he was already so close to the ground that he had absolutely no room for error. The helicopter began to buck and climb and dive without purpose.

Joanne heard what sounded like a couple of shots. They were not going to hurt Koya! Joanne did something she had never done before, something she did not even know she could do. The new part of her brain suddenly kicked in. She instinctively reached out to the two minds she could sense in the helicopter and began pulling strings. The helicopter came to an immediate halt in mid-air and fell directly to the desert floor. The rotor was still turning, but the helicopter wasn't moving.

Joanne just held tight to Molly and watched. She really didn't know what had happened. In a minute or two, Koya extracted himself from the mess in the cockpit and sat briefly on the edge of the window. Then he flew up, circled around a few times and took off into the sky.

Joanne, likewise, didn't wait around very long. She nudged Molly forward around the helicopter and the two headed off at a good trot to the southeast.

Gray Wolf was still mad as a wet hen. He had headed straight to Wakulla. On the way he ran into Red Hawk. She picked up on his temper.

"Who ruffled your feathers?" Red Hawk asked as they rode on together.

"What is the FBI and their fancy helicopters doing on the reservation?" he demanded. "They almost blinded me and my horse this morning."

"I don't know anything about any helicopters," Red Hawk answered. "I have been out at your cabin all weekend monitoring a Rockin'-R camper."

"They must be searching for that missing camper," Gray Wolf suggested. "Why were you monitoring the camper?"

"The girl was the daughter of Mary Gauss and Enela," Red Hawk explained. "She has some Elder characteristics and was going through puberty. She needed all the help I could give her."

"Where is she now?" Gray Wolf asked.

"On her way back to the Rockin'-R," Red Hawk explained. "I put her on the trail this morning."

"I hope she hasn't run afoul of that damn helicopter," was all Gray Wolf could muster.

The two rode on to Wakulla, stabled their horses and walked over to Billy's office. He was sitting in the back room fuming at the radio.

"What's up, Billy?" Red Hawk asked.

"A few minutes ago," Billy said, "I heard a radio call from the helicopter that said they had found the girl. How is that even possible, Red Hawk?"

Red Hawk paused before she answered. "I don't know, Billy," she eventually said. "I put her on the trail back to the Rockin'-R early this morning. I suppose they could have come upon her ... "

"They came upon me," Gray Wolf chimed in. "Almost spooked my horse!" I want that blasted thing off my reservation – now!"

"They won't be around any more if they actually found her," Billy stated flatly. "That's what I'm trying to find out now. I haven't heard anything since that partial message."

Just then, the front door of the office came open with a thud and a familiar voice sang out, "Sheriff!"

"Back here," Billy yelled. A moment later Walker came into the back room.

"What's going on?" he demanded to know. "I just got a message saying the helicopter had found the girl, then nothing."

"Same here," Billy concurred. "Do you think it could have crashed?"

"I'll get a crew out here immediately and check it out," Walker said.

Before he could leave, Billy called after him, "By the way, you're over-flight permit has just expired. Don't plan on replacing the helicopter."

Billy later learned that the helicopter had indeed crashed. Shots had been fired by the crew, but apparently nothing had been hit but the helicopter itself. The two crew members were found alive, but were in some sort of catatonic state. Until they could be interrogated, there was nothing left for the FBI to investigate.

Chapter 13

Back to the Ranch

Once Joanne had put some distance between her and the helicopter, she turned Molly due south at a steady walk. She was hoping to cross the trail the ranch hands had followed to Wakulla. She kept her eyes on the mountains to the east. She looked for the small gap between two sets of hills that they had originally passed through. After about two hours, Joanne found what looked to be the trail she wanted. She turned Molly toward the east and followed the trail. Now, she could breath a little easier.

Joanne kept Molly at a steady walk. While they were on relatively level ground, every so often she would nudge Molly into a canter, or even a trot, for a short period. Molly's condition was Joanne prime concern. Bill Thomas had coached them well on the trip to Wakulla. Joanne now had to recall that lesson.

Joanne was also concerned about food and water for Molly. She had brought no food with her except the jerky Red Hawk had given her. She did have the pouch of water; and she could use her hat as a bowl for Molly. Her only chance to refill her pouch would be rain or some natural source of water. Bill had taken them over a small stream on the way to Wakulla. But she would have to find the stream, and it would have to be flowing when she got to it.

It was beginning to cloud up in the heat of the day. But Joanne was riding away from the on-coming clouds. Maybe, if they moved in quickly …

A good hard rain would make life on horseback miserable, but it would solve the water problem.

Joanne stopped briefly for lunch and to give Molly some water. She let Molly search for something to eat, but the pickings were slim. Neither did the heat let up any. It was a competition between the slight cloud cover and the natural warming of the day. The clouds did help a little, but there was still no rain. After thirty minutes she was back in the saddle pressing on toward the Rockin'-R.

That afternoon there was a brief rain shower. Joanne turned her hat upside down to catch as much water as she could. When the shower petered out she stopped and let Molly drink as much of the water as she wanted.

The two kept on through the afternoon and into the early evening. At last they came upon the stream and it was indeed still flowing. Before she started making camp, Joanne led Molly to the stream and let her drink her fill. There was more vegetation near the water, so Joanne removed her saddle from Molly and let her forage.

Joanne went to the stream and filled her canteen. But the water looked too inviting after a hot day in the saddle. Joanne couldn't resist a quick dip in the icy water of the stream.

She climbed out soaking wet. She stripped off her wet clothes and hung them over some low braches of a nearby bush. She had nothing with which to dig a latrine, so she simply made due with a partially isolated spot.

Joanne ate more jerky for supper and washed it down with more stream water. By then darkness was rapidly descending. She located Molly and brought her back to the camp site by the stream. She decided to tie Molly up overnight – just in case.

Joanne found a suitable spot to bed down for the night. She removed the extra blanket from her saddle and laid it out. Then she stretched out on half of it, using the saddle as a pillow, and pulled the other half blanket over her. She was instantly asleep.

Joanne's sleep was again interrupted by dreams. She dreamed that she was back among the Elders in the butte. It was pleasant and comfortable to be among her own kind. No cares, no worries, plenty of food and water. It was almost like living in Eden. Why would they ever want to give up such a wonderful life? Her dream gave her no hint. She almost met Enela. Enela was approaching Joanne, but something else was happening.

Joanne was instantly awake. It was pitch dark. She glanced at he watch, but couldn't read the dial. She couldn't quite recall the dream. Why was she awake? She listened carefully. She could not detect any strange sound. Molly was moving a bit, but she didn't seem nervous. Joanne assessed her options.

There were no trees to climb. She had no weapons. It would take time to saddle Molly and ride off. Besides, Joanne did not relish trying to ride through strange country in the dark. There was only one thing to do: play possum.

Joanne slowly and quietly rolled up tightly in her blanket and did her best to lay perfectly still. She even quieted her breathing. But she kept her other senses on high alert. At first there was nothing. Then soft steps, breathing. Something was coming closer.

Her eyes would do her no good, so Joanne opened her mind. She could almost sense the wolf.

She sent a calm thought of greeting out to the wolf. Something akin to, "Hello, Brother Wolf".

The approaching steps stopped. Joanne could hear breathing; or was it sniffing? Then more steps receding into the distance.

Quiet returned to the little camp by the stream. Eventually, Joanne rolled over and slept soundly until dawn. The were no more dreams.

She was up with the sun. Some jerky, some water from the stream for her and for Molly. Then it was time to saddle up for the last leg of the ride to the Rockin'-R. Once she was mounted and on her way, Joanne checked her direction with her watch and took a slightly southeasterly course. The trail was clearer now and she had no doubt she would soon see the fence.

She did see the fence, but it was not until one o'clock in the afternoon. The fence was aligned north-south, so Joanne turned Molly to the north and had another twenty-minute ride to the gate. Once she was inside the gate, Joanne felt she had accomplished her mission. She remembered where the watering spots were and headed for the nearest one, where she let Molly have a well-deserved drink. Four hours later the stable was in sight and she picked up her pace.

Everything was quiet around the stable. The ranch hands were obviously still out on the range and there was little for Charlie to do. Joanne dismounted at the stable door and led Molly inside. She removed her saddle and put it on the rack designated for the ranch hands' use. Then Joanne prepared a large bag of oats for Molly, grabbed a curry brush and went after her with a vengeance while she devoured the oats. After the brushing, Joanne removed Molly's bridle, put a stable blanket on her and put her in a stall filled with fresh hay.

Before going to the bunkhouse, Joanne stopped by the dining hall. Eddie was not there, so she simply raided the kitchen for what food was left over. There wasn't much more than bread and peanut butter, but it was better than a steady diet of jerky.

Then she walked back to the bunkhouse. It also was empty and smelled somewhat musty from disuse. She didn't bother turning on any lights; there was still enough daylight for her purposes.

Joanne took off her clothes and stowed them away for washing – the sooner , the better. Next came the comfort of a real toilet and a nice long warm shower, with plenty of soap. Thoroughly refreshed, she made a bee-line for her top bunk and settled in for a decent night's sleep.

When we are awake, it sometimes requires much effort to set our minds free. And when we do so it is often to focus on a single concept or idea. When we sleep, our brains are set free and it is the brain that determines what it will focus on. We call such episodes 'dreams'. Pundits have said the dreaming is just the brain's way of emptying the trash. Wise men think that some dreams may be glimpses into our future. Sometimes we remember them when we wake, sometimes we don't. This night, as Joanne slept, she dreamed.

In her dream she revisited many of the things she had seen during her time at the Rockin'-R. She revisited the horses, but in her dream they were running free over the range. A large black one was leading the herd. They were racing free, this way and that. They were happy. Then her dream shifted to the cattle. There was a large fire surrounded by cowboys and cattle. But it was the cattle who were doing the branding, assuring the cowboys that the brand that seared their flesh was completely painless. They didn't agree and were doing their best to escape.

The cowboys and cattle around the fire were replaced by several wolves. The wolves circled the fire cautiously. Then they suddenly stood up on their hind legs and began dancing around it. The fire started to spin and rose up off the ground. The spinning fire morphed into a spinning centrifuge. The centrifuge receded into the background. It was in the back of a truck. The men in the truck were processing sperm that would be used to inseminate the cattle. One of the men doing the processing looked up and explained that one load of semen from a donor could be separated into dozens of separate inseminations. That message was repeated: Only a tiny amount of live sperm was necessary. One shot of semen could impregnate dozens; why waste it on a single recipient?

Sometimes, we remember our dreams.

Chapter 14

Where Have You Been?

Charlie actually lived a few miles from the Rockin-R in a little house with his wife and two kids. With the ranch hands out on the range, there wasn't a lot for Charlie to do around the stable. He still had to feed and tend the few horses that were kept there. He would came in at six in the morning, and turn the horses out into the corral for some exercise. Then he would clean out the stalls, make any repairs that were necessary, tend to the area around the stable and generally look after the place. In the afternoon, he would tend to the horses' needs. He could pretty much work at his leisure.

This particular morning was no exception. Charlie drove over to the ranch and parked his pick-up behind the stable. He came in the back door and began greeting the horses as usual. Then he stopped in his tracks. There, in what was supposed to be an empty stall was ... Charlie took a closer look: Molly!

When Bill had called in to the ranch to report that one of the ranch hands was missing in Wakulla, Mr. Rogers had contacted everyone on the ranch to see if they had any knowledge about the disappearance. Charlie knew that it was Joanne and Molly who were missing.

Charlie looked again at the horse in the 'empty' stall. Yes, it was Molly. "If Molly were back," Charlie thought, "maybe the girl was back, too." Charlie hurried back to the stall in the rear of the stable that served as his 'office' and picked up the intercom. "It may be early," Charlie mused, "but the boss needs to know about this."

Mrs. Rogers answered the intercom. "What is it, Charlie? It's awfully early for chit-chat."

"Sorry to bother you, Mrs. Rogers," Charlie began, "but I was wonderin' if you had any more news on the missing girl?"

"No, Charlie," she replied, somewhat upset at the early call. "I'm sure Mr. Rogers would have told you if there were any."

"Yes, ma'am," Charlie said quite politely. "Then could you please tell him when he wakes up that the girl's horse is back in the stable – in a stall – with a stable blanket on her. I just thought he might want to know."

"Charlie!" Mrs. Rogers almost shouted into the phone, "You stay right there on the line. I'll get Mr. Rogers."

Charlie liked Mr. Rogers; but he didn't care all that much for his wife. He held onto the phone with a slight smile on his face, licked his finger and made a single stroke in the air.

"Charlie!," Mr. Rogers didn't sound the least bit sleepy, "What were you saying about the missing girl's horse?"

"Good mornin', Sir," Charlie offered. "I was just sayin' that I found the girl's horse here in the stable when I arrived this morning. Horse didn't just wander in overnight. It had been groomed and fed, and there is a saddle and bridle hangin' on the ranch hands' tack rack."

"Any sign of the girl?" Mr. Rogers was sounding excited.

"Not here in the stable, Sir" Charlie was in good form this morning.

"Meet me at the bunkhouse in five minutes." The line went dead.

The bunkhouse was only three minutes – at the most – from the stable. Charlie proceeded to let the horses out into the corral as he headed to the front of the stable. He removed the stable blanket from Molly and turned her out with the others. Then he ambled up the hill toward the bunkhouse. He watched as he went and noticed Mr. Rogers coming down from the main house. He was wearing his usual plaid shirt, blue jeans and boots. Charlie opined that he could still run pretty good for an old man with some extra baggage to carry.

The two arrived at the front door of the bunkhouse at the same time. Charlie deferred to Mr. Rogers as to who would open the door and followed him inside. The sun was just rising over the mountains, so the interior was only dimly lit. The two men looked around. Neither knew which was the girl's bunk. In a moment, Charlie pointed down to their right. The top bunk appeared to be mussed up.

As though afraid of waking the dead, the two men moved slowly and quietly down the aisle to the girl's bunk. There was indeed a young girl sleeping peacefully on the top bunk. If that had been a boy, Mr. Rogers would have him up instantly and pleading for mercy. But, Mr. Rogers was loathe to reach up and touch a girl. He wanted no part of an improper touching lawsuit.

"Ahem!" Mr. Rogers said. The girl showed no signs of responding.

"AHEM!" he repeated several decibels louder.

Joanne woke and groggily looked for the source of the unwanted disturbance. When Joanne saw Mr. Rogers standing on the floor beside her bunk, grog instantly changed to panic and she sat bolt upright, staring down at him.

"Uh, good morning," she said.

"What in blue blazes are you doing up there?" Mr. Rogers demanded angrily.

"Ah, sleeping?" Joanne answered.

"Where have you been?" Mr. Rogers was no less angry.

"It' a long story," Joanne began. "I'd rather not have to repeat it more than once."

"You be in my office in ten minutes," Mr. Rogers demanded. "Charlie, you stick around and make sure she doesn't disappear again." He turned and left the bunkhouse. Charlie just stood there. He was a little unsure just what he was supposed to do at this point. He well knew that if the girl disappeared again while in his care, Mr. Rogers would hang him out to dry and simply forget he was on the clothesline.

Joanne picked up on Charlie's indecision. "You know," she said, "I do sleep in the nude. Do I get a little privacy to get dressed?"

"Yeah, sure," Charlie said. But he wasn't at all sure. He wasn't even sure that she did indeed sleep in the nude. She might be fully clothed right now, just waiting for another chance to run off. Finally, he just said, "I'll stand back here." And moved back to a spot near the front door.

Joanne lost no time. She reached down and opened the far door on her locker. Then she hopped down from the top bunk, using the open door as a shield, grabbed a towel, shirt, jeans and socks, panties and boots. With these in hand she rolled over the lower bunk and ducked into the latrine area.

She turned on the closest shower and quickly rinsed off, using the shower as a handy urinal. When she was done, she turned the cold water off and the hot water on full. While the stem built up she dried and quickly dressed. Then, waving the steam towards the door, she used it as a smokescreen and slipped through the outside door of the latrine and hid around the corner of the bunkhouse.

Charlie had been patiently waiting back in the bunkhouse. When he saw the steam, he became curious. When it persisted, he became nervous. He called out to Joanne, who remained as silent as she could while stifling a laugh.

Charlie gave up. "I'm comin' in," he announced and made his way to the latrine. He cautiously peeked in, trying to brush away the steam. He made his way to the shower and turned it off. He looked around; Joanne wasn't there. Now real panic set in. Charlie rushed outside to the troughs and looked some more. Still no Joanne. He turned left and looked around the back of the building. No Joanne in sight anywhere. He turned and went to the front of the building. No Joanne.

Charlie was in full panic mode. How had she managed to escape? He was almost spinning in circles trying to catch a glimpse of her. At one point, he thought he caught sight of a shadow moving inside the bunkhouse. He ran back into the bunkhouse through the latrine. No Joanne.

Poor Charlie. He just knew his nice life on the ranch was over. He slowly made his way back to the front door and exited the bunkhouse, wondering what in the world he was going to tell Mr. Rogers.

Joanne was leaning against one of the posts that held up the roof over the entry. "Well, really," she snickered, "what kept you? We're going to have to hurry or we'll be late." She was holding her hat in her hands twirling it gently. Charlie went through several shades from simple anger to rage to frustration.

"Sorry," Joanne admitted, "I forgot my hat and had to go back for it. Shall we?" She started off up the path to the ranch house.

The two made short work of the walk to Mr. Rogers' office. Charlie knocked on the screen when they arrived and they both walked in. Mr. Rogers was sitting at his desk waiting for them.

"Well, I'm happy to see that you two made it," he greeted them. "Joanne, your mother has been staying at a nearby motel. She should be here in about fifteen minutes. A representative from the FBI will also be here shortly. The are very curious as to why their new sophisticated electronic surveillance system couldn't find any trace of you. For some strange reason, the sheriff over in Wakulla wasn't interested in the least. Any reason you can think of, for that?"

Joanne hesitated a moment, then said, "No. No reason I can think of."

"Charlie," Mr. Rogers said, "you can go back to work now. And thank you for your help."

Charlie nodded and fled the office. He certainly had his fill of this particular ranch hand.

Joanne's mother was the first to arrive. Joanne could identify the sound of her car as she pulled into the parking lot. She counted her steps on the gravel as her mother approached the door. Then Joanne scrunched down in her seat, stretched out her legs and pulled her hat down over her eyes.

Mary didn't bother knocking. She just pulled the screen door open as she came to it. She was wearing a plain white blouse and a pair of tight-fitting red capris. She spotted Joanne slouched in her seat and walked directly over to her. Mr. Rogers watched her entrance with some interest.

"Don't pull that old cow poke act on me, young lady," Mary began. "Just where have you been?"

Joanne pushed the hat back and straightened in her seat. "Let's just wait until the whole audience is here, mom" she suggested. "It's a long story and I really don't want to keep repeating it all day."

Mr. Rogers looked up at Mary and just shrugged. "Might as well," he said. "The FBI is on their way."

Mary resigned herself to the inevitable and settled in the chair next to Joanne. Once she was seated, she leaned over and whispered, "This had better be good!"

Ten minutes later there was a clatter outside. Mr. Rogers rose and went to the door. "Looks like the FBI is here," he said and returned to his seat. He looked over at Mary and Joanne, "They came by helicopter." he informed them.

A few minutes later a tallish man in a dark blue suit walked into the office. He was middle aged but still very fit and trim. He spotted Mr. Rogers seated at the desk and went directly over to him. He quickly flashed a badge and id card; "Walker, FBI," he announced.

Mr. Rogers bade him sit in the chair opposite Joanne. Then all eyes descended on Joanne.

"Well, young lady," Mr. Rogers said. "Let's have it."

Joanne just gulped. She knew this would have to be convincing. No errors. So she decided to make it irrefutably convincing.

"It's like this," she said, and attempted to connect with the other three minds in the room just as she had connected with the wolf.

"I was feeling the onset of my first period as we approached Wakulla. I went to the general store to get something, like pads and maybe some Midol. Being in the saddle for hours was not helping the pain and discomfort. But I couldn't find anything in the store. I didn't know what to do, so I guess I just panicked. I didn't want to be around the guys, just bleeding through my pants. And I really didn't want to endure that long ride back to the Rockin'-R on Sunday. So I just saddled up Molly and headed out to find some place I could hole up for the duration. I rode north out of Wakulla into the hills until I found a nice deep cave with a water source.

"I rested there for a few days until the bleeding stopped. I didn't know where the other ranch hands were by then, so I rode back here. I got here late yesterday afternoon. I really wanted a shower and a good night's sleep. You woke me up this morning. That's all there is to it."

"But we searched the hills north of the town," Walker insisted. We couldn't find any trace of you or this cave you say you were in."

"I heard the helicopter, buzzing around in the distance," Joanne explained. "But you never got over to my cave. I made sure that Molly and I were well inside the cave when you were around." She made a more urgent effort to convince Walker of her good intentions.

"Well, I for one completely believe her," Mr. Rogers announced. He was rather credulous and not a big believer in the fancy gadgets the Government was using. He got a bit of a disgusted look from Walker.

Mary sat there in silence. She was reserving judgment. She believed she would soon have Joanne captive in her car for the trip back to Albuquerque. That would be time enough to get to the bottom of this.

Joanne's creative coaching was working. Everyone just sat there for a moment. Then Walker stood up. "Well, as incredible as it seems," he said, "I guess I have what I need to finish my report. The missing child has been found and returned to her mother." Then he turned to Mary.

"I trust you are satisfied now that your child is back, however it happened." It wasn't a questions, exactly, but he waited for a response.

"Yes, I guess I am," Mary responded. The comment was directed to both Mr. Walker and Mr.

Rogers. The latter was especially glad that there would be no law suit over this fiasco.

Walker shook hands with Mr. Rogers, turned and walked out the door. A few minutes later the helicopter could be heard taking off from a nearby pasture.

Mary turned to Joanne. "Now what?" she asked bluntly.

"Maybe I just ought to go back home," Joanne said. "Before I get into more trouble," she added quickly.

Mary turned to Mr. Rogers. "Is that agreeable to you?" she asked.

"Yes, of course," he answered. "But then there is the matter of the fee ... " He left the end of the sentence dangling.

"Well, we have put you to a good deal of effort and expense," Mary responded. "Why don't we just let the matter rest?"

"Perfectly acceptable," Mr. Rogers agreed.

"Now, young lady," Mary directed. "Suppose you go pack up your stuff and bring it up to the car. I'll wait for you here."

Joanne moved quickly out the door and headed for the bunkhouse at a good jog.

Chapter 15

Home to Albuquerque

Joanne's first stop was the stable to get her saddle. On the way back to the bunkhouse, she stopped by the corral to say good-bye to Molly. Joanne really liked the little roan. She had been a good companion. Joanne shared a special thought with her; and got a special thought back in return. Then she headed back to the bunkhouse.

Packing the duffle bag was easy. Joanne just grabbed everything that was hers and stuffed it in, clean and dirty alike. It could all be sorted out when she got home. With saddle and duffle bag in tow she returned to the car where her mother and Mr. Rogers were waiting.

Joanne stowed her duffle bag and saddle in the car. Then she turned and said good-bye to Mr. Rogers and the Rockin'-R, and thanked him for … whatever. She and her mother got in the car and began the drive back to Albuquerque.

Once they were on the interstate, following the northbound traffic, Mary glanced over at her daughter and said, "Okay, I'm not about to accept that crazy menstruation story for another minute. What really happened in Wakulla?"

"Well," Joanne began, "the pain factor was real. I had been having headaches and belly aches for several days before the Wakulla trip. And they were getting worse. Bobbi knew about them.

"Why didn't you ask for help while you were at the ranch?" Mary asked.

"I don't know," Joanne replied. "Somehow it just didn't seem like I was supposed to. As it turned out, both of us would have been in a whole lot of trouble if I had.

"Anyway, I had to stop on the trail just before we got to Wakulla, just to let the pain subside. When we finally got to Wakulla, I did go to the general store to get something for the pain. But, I guess, I was hit with another bout of pain while I was there. The next thing I remember clearly was waking up in Gray Wolf's cabin a few days later."

"Who is this, 'Gray Wolf'," Mary asked suspiciously.

"Gray Wolf is a tribal shaman," Joanne answered. "But he wasn't there. I never did get to meet him."

"Well," Mary asked, "just how did you get from the general store to the cabin? And just how many days did you spend there."

"I think I spent three days there," Joanne counted out on her fingers. "No, four," she corrected. "Sunday, Monday, Tuesday and Wednesday. The only days I really remember are part of Tuesday and Wednesday."

"So you were unconscious for two and a half days?" Mary was incredulous. "Personally I am beginning to like your cave story better."

"It was on Wednesday," Joanne explained, "that I learned what had been going on and why. I agree, without the information my caregiver gave me, this would sound like some sort of a fairy tale."

124

"Just who was your 'caregiver'?" Mary asked, too casually for her own good.

"Another tribal shaman," Joanne quietly said, "by the name of Red Hawk."

That name got Mary's attention, but she couldn't quite remember where she had heard it. "Red Hawk?" she mumbled.

"Well," Joanne mused, "here's another name that you might remember: Enela."

It took Mary almost thirty seconds to regain control over her SUV, after scaring the pants off of two truckers and three other cars – and attracting the attention of a state trooper.

His flashing blue lights got Mary's attention and she obediently pulled over to the side of the road.

Mary produced the required documentation and explained to the young, nice looking trooper that she had just been momentarily startled by something her daughter said, and no, officer, it would not happen again. He grudgingly forgave her for briefly driving recklessly and suggested that they abstain from startling conversations while they were on the road. Mary took a few minutes to get her composure back and then resumed her trip. The trooper followed for a bit and then turned off the interstate.

Mary's curiosity was now bubbling over. "What do you know about, Enela?" she asked.

"Not very much," Joanne admitted. "But I do know that you and Enela were lovers."

Mary dug her fingernails into the steering wheel and tensed her muscles so tightly that she almost forgot to breathe. "What in the world ever gave you that absurd idea?" she blurted out.

"Red Hawk told me everything," Joanne continued her story. "She was called in when I collapsed in the general store. She recognized my problem and knew what to do from past experience. She and Sheriff Billy Eagle devised a plan to fake out anyone who might subsequently be on my trail. Then they took me to Gray Wolf's cabin where she managed to solve my problem."

"What, exactly, was your 'problem'?" Mary asked.

"Puberty." Joanne answered.

"That's ridiculous!" Mary retorted. "You aren't yet old enough."

"I would be if I were an Elder," Joanne totally destroyed Mary's mind.

"You are not an Elder," Mary sputtered. "You are a human. I gave birth to you." Mary was almost in panic mode. She had been so relieved when Joanne was born; she appeared so normal, so human.

"Not quite," Joanne interrupted Mary's reverie. "I look human on the outside, but inside I am mostly Elder. That was what was wrong; I was going through Elder puberty. If Red Hawk had not intervened, I would either have been driven mad or died."

Mary slowly pulled over to the side of the road. She silently looked at Joanne for a minute and the totally broke own in tears. Joanne could not quite fathom what Mary was thinking, but she knew how to resolve the situation. She reached tentatively into Mary's mind and made a few tiny adjustments.

In another few moments, the tears stopped and Mary sat up, not really sure why, but her crying jag was over.

"Then this puberty problem is completely over, now?" Mary asked as she composed herself to continue the journey.

"Yes, completely," Joanne replied. "In Elder terms I am now an adult. But I am afraid I shall have to be somewhat careful around humans. They will still see me as just another little girl.

Mary glanced over at her daughter and carefully moved the car back onto the interstate. "Just how much did Red Hawk tell you?" she asked again, bracing herself for what she feared would come.

"As I said," Joanne answered, "she just told me about Enela and how I was half Elder and where you got all you money – about the lottery number. There wasn't enough time for much more.

On Thursday morning, I got on Molly and Red Hawk led me away from the cabin and put me on the trail back to the Rockin'-R. I did have run-in with the FBI search helicopter on the way, but Red Hawk's spirit guide took care of that little problem. Then that night on the trail I seem to recall a brief conversation with a wolf – but that might have just been a dream. I'm not sure."

"Spirit guide?" Mary thought this was getting just a bit spooky.

"Every shaman," Joanne explained, "has a spirit guide. Red Hawk's is a falcon. When I ran into the helicopter, her falcon dove into the cockpit and caused the helicopter to crash. I helped by putting the two crew members to sleep before they could kill the bird."

Mary suddenly had a horrible thought. "Can you read minds?" She asked.

"No, not really," Joanne replied. "Sometimes I can influence humans. But I am just beginning to work out what I can do, and how to do it."

"Did you 'influence' me a while back?"

"Yes, a little bit," Joanne confessed. "I'm sorry, but you appeared to be in such pain, that I simply couldn't allow it to continue."

"I want you to promise right now that you will never do that again," Mary demanded quite sternly.

"I promise," Joanne said softly. "But I have a favor to ask, too."

"Yes?" Mary acknowledged, almost too casually.

"For now on," Joanne said, "I would like to be called, 'Elena'. It has more of an Elder character to it. Don't you think?"

The rest of the trip back to Albuquerque was not spent in silence. But there was no more conversation regarding what had transpired at Wakulla. Both Mary and Elena were deeply engaged with their own thoughts.

Epilogue

When Red Hawk had finished her tale, she sat in silence for a minute or two. Then she continued.

"When the Elders left the Earth, I thought that the situation had been completely resolved. Now, with the sudden appearance of Enela's daughter, the situation is no longer resolved at all. In fact the situation had re-emerged in a much more complex form.

"At that point I could not tell how the future would work out. But I feared that whatever happened would not be good for the humans or the Elders. It was bad enough when all of the Elders were living in the butte on the reservation under the protection of a shaman.

"I remember how badly it often went when a few Elders left their safe home here to live among the humans. Even in those few case, they went in pairs so that they had companionship and some safety in numbers. Now a young Elder was out in the human world alone. I feared she would not fit in with the human world; and there was no Elder world for her to retreat back into.

I tried to keep in touch with her. I found her Face-Book page and sent her a few email messages. Occasionally she would reply. But her replies were so general, that they gave me no clue as to what was actually happening in her life or how she was feeling.

I did learn that her mother had completed her nursing program and was looking for a position.

Then the Face-Book page went away. The emails were returned. I lost all contact with her.

I returned to my simple life with my husband, Sam, sharing my time between being Red Hawk on the reservation and Dr. Joanne Archer at the Winton hospital.

Red Hawk closed her eyes. The lesson was over.

== 30 ==

Also by Robyn Kelly:

The Elder Chronicles: The Lost World
The Elder Chronicles: Birth of a Savior
The Elder Chronicles: Elder Child
The Elder Chronicles: The Legend of Red Hawk
The Elder Chronicles: Elder Escape

Watch for volume seven of
The Elder Chronicles: Elena's Plan
Coming Soon!